P9-DNB-382

City Boy

Jan Michael

Clarion Books
Houghton Mifflin Harcourt
Boston   New York
2009

Clarion Books
215 Park Avenue South, New York, NY 10003
Copyright © 2008 by Jan Michael
First published in the United Kingdom in 2008 by Andersen Press, Ltd.
First American edition, 2009.

Clarion Books is an imprint of Houghton Mifflin Harcourt Publishing Company.

www.clarionbooks.com

Printed in the United States of America.

Library of Congress Cataloging-in-Publication Data

Michael, Jan.
[Leaving home]
City boy / Jan Michael. — 1st American ed.
p. cm.
Summary: In the southern African country of Malawi, after the AIDS-related deaths
of both of his parents, a boy leaves his affluent life in the city to live in a rural village,
sharing a one-roomed hut with his aunt, his cousins, and other orphans.
ISBN 978-0-547-22310-0
[1. Orphans—Fiction. 2. Country life—Malawi—Fiction. 3. Blacks—Malawi—Fiction.
4. Malawi—Fiction.] I. Title.

PZ7.M5796Ci 2009
[Fic]—dc22
2008037418

QUM 10 9 8 7 6 5 4 3 2 1

For Mercy Maliro
and for Bastiaan Sizoo

THE DEEP HOLE AT SAM'S FEET GAPED UP AT HIM. THE
smell of newly dug earth enveloped him, damp and cool and
musty as it rose from the pit. A pile of the African soil, the
color of blood, was heaped up on the right, drying in the
afternoon heat. Sam took a long, shuddering breath.

People were seated on the ground around; some, like
him, under the clump of trees at the head of the pit. At his
side, a woman began to sing, her voice low and soft. A second
woman's voice joined the first, and then another woman's,
then a man's and another man's, till the singing was all
around Sam, in the trees and among the graves.

Sam didn't sing. He didn't open his mouth. He stared
down at his feet. He was wearing the running shoes that his
mother had given him for his birthday, eight months ago.
They were bright blue, and red lights flashed round the heels
when he moved. They were for special, she'd said. He'd made
a secret vow to the carving of a squatting man that had been
in the corner of his room for as long as he could remember. "I
shan't wear them," he'd told the figure, crouching down to
its level, "till her cough is better." Every night he'd raised the
shoes from their box and stroked the new leather before
replacing them in the darkness under his bed. He'd kept to

his vow—except once, when he'd slipped them on and walked through into the living room, enjoying the sparkle of their lights in the darkness, but that didn't count.

He winced. He'd never worn them since, not till now. Her cough had gotten worse. Now he was wearing them in her honor. Eight months ago they'd actually been a bit big for him—"So that they'll last a while," she'd said. They had lasted, but she hadn't.

They fitted him now. If he stared at them, he wouldn't have to look down into the empty pit. If he stared at them, he might not cry. If he'd invented special occasions before and worn them and not waited, would she still be alive?

Beside him, four men grunted as they maneuvered a large, long wooden box above the hole. They began lowering it on thick ropes down into the earth.

Sam watched as a hot ray of sunlight pierced the canopy of leaves above and hit the polished wood of the coffin, making it gleam and flash.

"I am the resurrection and the life. Whoever has faith in me shall live, even though he dies," read the minister in a loud voice from his small black book.

The coffin rocked. It banged against the side of the pit and stuck there at an angle. One of the men stamped on the corner. It budged a little, but not enough. Another man stamped on it, and the other three pushed and shoved to make it fit. It broke free at last and continued down into the pit. They lowered it faster now.

Sam stared at the coffin as it moved farther down, away from him.

His mother was in there. His *amai*.

His throat tightened so hard that he couldn't swallow. Blood raced to his head. Amai! The tears sprang from his eyes and tore down his cheeks as if they couldn't get out fast enough.

Mr. Gunya, his father's cousin, was speaking, but Sam wasn't listening. He was remembering how Amai had said he could wear the running shoes for special occasions. This wasn't what she'd meant. She'd baked him a cake, with green icing for a soccer field and white markings and a little goal at either end. He'd had his friends round at the weekend, but his birthday had been the next day. When he'd come home from school on Monday, she'd been waiting for him with that cake and his present.

She'd been so pretty. She'd gotten thinner, too. She'd said it was fashionable, being "slim," like the models in the European magazines she sometimes bought as a treat. Her eyes had glittered—he remembered that. But she'd gone on getting thinner, and weaker. She'd barely left her bed at the end, not till she died.

"Our sister Martha has gone forth upon her journey . . ." Everyone was silent, listening to the clergyman in his long robe.

How could Amai be going on any journey?

How could Amai be in that box?

Sam had seen her die, he'd been there, he'd been with her. He had known that the Disease had weakened her and that she had died of the coughing. She had explained it to him. Besides, he had already seen it with his father, three years before.

But what was death? One moment she was his amai and she was coughing and breathing. The life was in her. The next she stopped breathing, and you could see that the life was gone, that *she* was gone. *Pfff!* Like that. Blown away. Vanished. Her body was there, getting colder and stiffer, but that wasn't Amai, that wasn't his amai. It was only a shell left behind. So where was Amai? She had escaped, abandoning him.

People were standing up and coming closer. A woman nudged Sam. "You have to throw in some soil."

Sam stared at her, not understanding.

"The soil. There at the side. We're waiting for you."

Obediently, he bent to the pile of earth, but it wasn't really him who was feeling the warm soil, it wasn't really him who clutched a handful. It wasn't really him who swung his hand over the top of the pit and dropped the soil on the coffin lid and heard it land there on the wood like a patter of early rain. It was some other Sam.

The men who'd lowered the coffin dug their spades into the earth and sent it thundering down onto the wood, spade after spade, working energetically, their arms and shoulders gleaming with sweat. They went on until a mound of earth covered the place where the pit had been, the box where Amai lay, where Amai's body lay.

Everyone sang another hymn.

Then hands reached out and threw on flowers and wreaths till the heap was covered in pinks and reds and purples.

"Strengthen us now to live in the power of the resurrection, and keep us united with our loved one . . ."

All bowed their heads as the minister led them in another prayer.

Sam stared at the flowers, their petals already wilting in the heat of the afternoon.

Amai wasn't under those. She wasn't in that pit. How could she be?

2

"SAM MUST GO TO THE ORPHAN FARM."

With his ear pressed to the other side of the closed door, Sam recognized the voice. It belonged to Mr. Gunya, Sam's father's cousin. Mr. Gunya was a lawyer—a big man in town, not just in weight—and he had a big shiny car with a chauffeur. He always spoke loudly and slowly to make sure that everyone listened. Sam could just imagine him pushing out his belly as he held forth.

"That way Sam will still be in town, and he can continue to go to school."

"To Thint Mungo'th Thchool?" The woman's voice had a lisp. It was his mother's friend. "It ith an expenthive thchool."

A rumble of agreement came from the throats of the others gathered on the other side of the door.

"Who will pay the feeth?" went on the lisping voice.

"Not the estate." Mr. Gunya had been there all day studying papers, collecting bills and certificates, moving from one room to another, examining furniture and ornaments, gazing up at the ceiling.

He'd sent Sam out of his way. "Go and play," he'd ordered. So in his mother's office next door, Sam had turned on the computer and fiddled with Invaders 3, his favorite game, but his fingers wouldn't do what he wanted them to do. He felt sick. He missed Amai. He couldn't concentrate.

Now, yet again, he felt drawn to the door and the conference going on in the living room. It was the day after the funeral. He wanted to find out what he could about what was going on.

"There is nothing left in the estate from my cousin's business, only debts." Sam heard Mr. Gunya clear his throat. "After he died, I made every effort to aid his good lady, but she refused my advice. Clearly, the business was too much for the boy's mother to manage."

"She wath not well."

"Indeed. As I say, there is nothing." Mr. Gunya paused, and cleared his throat again. "I might point out that there is a perfectly good local school not far from the orphan farm."

7

"Please . . ."

It was his aunt's voice. His country aunt.

"We have a school in our village. Many children go there. My children go there, and they are happy. Sam can go to the village school. It is the village where his mother, my older sister, is from. It is right."

"Those children in village schools, they do not even have enough pencils to write with," said Mr. Gunya.

No pencils? *Well,* thought Sam, *never mind.* Sometimes he and his classmates typed straight onto the computer. His neck was beginning to ache from bending down at the keyhole. He dropped into a squat instead.

"Sir . . ." His aunt seemed to be ignoring the interruption. She must be appealing to the neighbors as well now, he thought. "Sam will be happy at the village school, and there are no fees to be paid. It is free. Sam will be fine with me and the other children. And I am family, too."

"Samuel Sangala is a city boy. Where do you live again?" As if Mr. Gunya didn't know!

"Mandingwe," said his aunt.

"Mandingwe. Quite so. It is out in the bush, many miles from here. Your nephew has been brought up to expect better. He has always lived here in town. He has been having a good education, he has smart clothes, he is used to television and computers. His parents have brought him up the modern way. They are buried here, too, in the modern way."

"I am aware of that. But it is not right. She should have come back to the village to be buried with her ancestors." His aunt's voice went very low. There was a long, drawn-out silence. Sam heard her sigh. "And now you are telling us that there is no money. So is not family better than orphan farm? Or perhaps you will take him into your home here in town?" After all, Mr. Gunya was family, too; he was the one in charge.

Sam held his breath. He didn't want to live with Mr. Gunya. Mrs. Gunya was as wide as he was. They had no children of their own, and their house was large and dark, with big furniture that children were not allowed to sit on and a garden with flowers that children were not allowed to pick. They probably wouldn't even let him have friends over.

He waited, sweating, in the silence that followed. A large black ant that had been crawling up his shoe reached the edge and came onto his leg. It tickled. He reached down to brush it off. The ant bit him. "Ow!"

Footsteps strode toward the door, and before Sam could move away, it was yanked open. The lawyer stood in the opening, almost blocking it. From behind him, Sam's mother's friend and her husband, and the neighbor and his wife, and his aunt gazed at him, as if for the first time. He knew what they were looking at. They saw a sturdy boy standing squarely in front of them, his face grubby from crying, his skin gleaming from nerves as much as from sweat. The short-sleeved white shirt he'd put on, thinking he would be going to school, was wrinkled, and his khaki shorts were in need of a wash. Amai hadn't been there the night before to tell him not to crumple them and chuck them on the floor, she hadn't been there to remind him to wear clean shorts. She hadn't been there. He'd slipped away from the end of the funeral meal, all that drinking and talking, and put himself to bed—without brushing his teeth, he remembered guiltily.

He gazed back at them blankly. Since Amai had died, he had felt peculiar inside, all empty. Each morning when he woke up, the day looked just the same, the sky blue and fresh, the rooster two houses down crowing as usual. But he no longer knew what to expect.

"Hrrumph," grunted Mr. Gunya. "I suppose you may as well come in and listen here as listen at the door." He moved aside. "After all, it is your future that concerns us."

Behind him, Aunt Mercy held out her arms. Sam left the shelter of the doorway and went to her and let her hold him. The shiny buckle of her belt dug into his side, but even so it was comforting to be hugged. Amai had hugged him all the time.

From inside Aunt Mercy's arms, he gazed down at her skirt. His mother would have turned up her nose at the bright colors, as she would have at her younger sister's hair. It was tight and curly and simple, like his. Aunt Mercy hadn't grown her hair and had it straightened every week, as Amai used to. She smelled different from Amai, too, sort of salty and smoky.

When Aunt Mercy turned up at the funeral, Sam barely remembered her. He'd met her only once before, when she and his uncle had arrived on the doorstep and said they were coming to stay the night, maybe the week. They lived too far away to come to town often, Amai had explained to Sam, and, when he'd said he wanted to meet his cousins as well, she'd reminded him that there were three of them, which made it too expensive for the family to travel.

So why couldn't he and Amai go to the village to meet

them? Amai had given a great gurgling laugh. "Me? Sleep in a mud hut again? No, those days are over, thank goodness," she said. "It isn't even as if there's a hotel there." And so they had never gone. "We want the best for you," he could remember his father saying. "Those people in the bush are ignorant." When Atate had said that, Amai had sucked her teeth, *"Tssk!"* but she hadn't contradicted him. "They're welcome to come here," she'd said. The cousins never had.

Now it looked as if Sam might be going there and meeting his cousins after all. *A mud hut?* Sam thought. He didn't especially want to sleep in one of those, either, but that was apparently what Aunty was offering.

The neighbor, a kind man who had often let Sam play with his collection of lead soldiers, crossed his legs. "In my opinion . . ." He stopped, looked nervously at Mr. Gunya, uncrossed his legs, sat up a bit straighter, and began again. "In my opinion, the boy should be with family. Charity should begin at home," he added hastily.

His wife, sitting beside him, thin and scrawny, smoking cigarette after cigarette, nodded vigorously.

Mr. Gunya looked put out. "If Samuel is to make something of himself, he must continue to go to school, preferably at St. Mungo's, and he must stay in town," he said firmly, "with the orphans."

The grownups exchanged glances. Sam felt relieved that Mr. Gunya hadn't said Sam would go to live with him and

Mrs. Gunya. But Sam didn't want to live with the orphans. "I can stay here," he suggested hopefully, "in this house."

Mr. Gunya snorted. "Don't be silly. You can't live on your own. You're far too young."

"Will you pay the thchool feeth, then, for Thint Mungo'th?" asked Amai's friend again.

Mr. Gunya frowned heavily. "My wife and I cannot possibly pay the fees of every boy in town who is orphaned," he said. "The funeral was a great drain on our resources. Apart from which, we have a very great number of other commitments and obligations. There are scholarships. Let the boy apply for one of those."

"Sam is not just 'every boy,'" muttered Aunty. She glared at Mr. Gunya. "He is your cousin's son. He is your duty."

Mr. Gunya showed no sign of having heard.

The neighbor shifted on his seat. "Perhaps family and a village school would be just as good as orphan farm and local city school."

"Better, I imagine," said Amai's friend in an undertone. "Bethides, it ith the custom. It ith good to keep to the old wayth. Even if thome of us do not." She frowned at Mr. Gunya.

Mr. Gunya sighed, a sigh that came from the bottom of that big belly and quivered upward to be released in a long breath. "Orphan or no orphan, I have business to attend to. An urgent town council meeting," he added, to make sure they understood just how valuable his time was. "I cannot remain here all morning arguing. You have heard my views. If you choose to ignore them in favor of tradition and custom, it is your right. I do not think that we should always follow custom nowadays. Nor did my cousin, the boy's father. But we live in a democracy; your opinion is your right.

"I shall send someone to pick up the computer," he went on as he gathered up his papers and turned to go. "My wife needs another for her lingerie business."

Sam stiffened. "The computer's mine now! Amai always let me use it."

"Ah." Mr. Gunya paused. "Perhaps one of you will explain." With that, he swept out.

Explain what? Sam ran back into the office and stood with his back to the computer, protecting it.

His aunt hoisted herself from the chair and came to stand in the doorway. "How does a computer work?" she asked him gently.

Sam stared at her. Perhaps no one in her village knew how to work a computer. He smiled for the first time that day. He would be able to show them. He could introduce them to computer games and things. "You press this button"—he pressed it off and then on again—"and it comes on. Then . . ."

"Yes, dear. But how does a computer start?"

He was puzzled. She must be ignorant, too, as his father

had said. He didn't say that, though. It would be disrespectful.

"It needs electricity," she pointed out. "We have no electricity."

No electricity? Sam's arms dropped to his sides in disbelief. Then he raised his head and shouted, "I'm staying here! I hate you!" and burst into tears.

At once she reached out for him and held him tightly.

"I know it's hard," she said, cuddling him to her. "Things will be very different for you now. But you will have me. And the children are longing to see you."

3

So it was settled. Sam was to go to Mandingwe with his aunt to live with her and his cousins.

"What a lot of clothes," Aunt Mercy commented as Sam pulled them out of drawers the next day. "Enock will be pleased. He is much the same size as you are. And Macdonald—the shirts might even fit him."

The same size, Enock? Or Macdonald? Enock was his cousin, but who was the other boy? Sam paused, frowning, about to fling a couple of T-shirts onto the bed, where his aunt was putting them into a suitcase.

"Ezelina, too." She held up a shirt thoughtfully. "You will learn to share with the others. They all do. Oh, come here," she said as the tears sprang to his eyes. "There, now." She wiped them away. "It is not important. We are talking only about clothes. But you have all these, and Enock and Ezelina have half a school uniform each, and then two shirts and a skirt for Ezelina between them. You'd want to share with your cousins and the others, wouldn't you?"

Sam nodded. What she said sounded right, he knew that. But they were his clothes, not hers. An angry knot began to tie itself deep inside him. It was Amai's fault for dying! His lips twisted. He turned away from his aunt and went on helping to pick out what to take. He'd never had to share; his friends all had clothes of their own.

He took off his ordinary sneakers and put them in the case, swapping them for his blue running shoes.

Running shoes? It was his first journey out of town. That was a special occasion. They'd be right for it. Also, it'd show his cousins that they were his and not for sharing. *Enock and Ezelina,* he thought. He knew they were twins, and he imagined that they would block him out like a wall. He felt nervous about meeting them. Who "the others" were, he had no idea. Not his uncle, anyway; he had died.

One large suitcase and a big bag later, they were finished. "We have an hour till the bus leaves. I'm going to make myself a cup of tea and sit outside on the stoop to drink it." Aunty bustled to the door. "I'll fetch a juice for you. Why don't you go round the house to make sure you've got everything you want, and then come and join me before we leave for the bus station?"

Sam trailed into his parents' bedroom—or, rather, into Amai's room. He sat on the bed. It had been hers alone since Atate had died. He could smell her there, smell the powder she puffed on in the morning to make her skin look paler, smell the expensive foreign perfume she dabbed on her wrists. He went over to her dressing table with its ruched curtains and glass top and saw the hairs trapped in her wide, long-toothed comb. She hadn't sat at the dressing table in the last weeks of her dying, hadn't left the bed. Someone had put a pretty flowered cover over the bed, where she had lain coughing and coughing till Sam had thought she would split in two, and he had wished she would stop. She had. Now he wished he could hear the noise once more.

Sam had pushed the bed closer to the window when she'd asked him to. She wanted to be in the shade spread by the mango tree outside. She liked the way it darkened and cooled the room, and she liked hearing the birds that sang their morning song from it just before the break of dawn. It had reminded her of her childhood, in the village where he was now going.

A village where he had never been, which Amai had refused to return to and had rarely spoken of until those last weeks when she lay dying. Then the things she had told him about it had sounded good, things like having lots of space to roam and storytelling round the fire after supper. For a moment his heart lifted, remembering. He got up from the bed and left the room.

In the office he went over to the computer and turned it on. He sat down, reaching out for a familiar game to slot in.

"Sam? Are you nearly done?" Aunty was calling him. "The bus leaves in twenty minutes."

Reluctantly, he turned the computer off again. He hit it with his fist, putting all his force behind it. "You're mine! Don't work for that Mrs. Gunya. Stay off!" He wrenched its plug out from the wall. That made him feel a little better. Turning his back on it, he surveyed the room.

A couple of minutes later he joined Aunty on the stoop, carrying a silver-framed photograph of his parents at their wedding. His father stood tall in a dark blue suit, looking straight at the camera. His mother, her hair straightened and stiffened for the first time in city fashion, was dressed in white satin from top to toe, and was looking shyly out.

Sam had always liked the photograph. It came from a time before he was born, a time when Amai and Atate had known each other before they had known him and before he had known them. It was before he existed. Amai had wanted brothers and sisters for him, but after his father had died of the Disease and she found out that she had it, too, she'd called him from the yard and pulled him to her. "God knew what He was doing when He gave me only one boy," she'd said. And now Sam existed, and his parents didn't.

"Ready?" Aunt Mercy stood up. She picked up his suitcase. "You bring the bag." She nodded toward it.

By the time they reached the bus stop and joined the queue of those already waiting, Sam's arm was aching from the weight of the bag. Among other things, it had his sneakers and flip-flops in it, his two favorite books and a Game Boy, and tins of food from the kitchen that Aunt Mercy had found and added.

The bus, when it came, was just a large van with an enclosed cab and an open back. Two wooden benches, screwed to the floor, ran down the sides. These were already fully occupied. A man, seeing Aunty, got up and offered her a place. Sam stood near her, clutching onto the metal struts that crossed the van as if supporting an invisible roof.

He had a great view as they drove slowly through town. He'd never been so high up before and able to look down on familiar sights; he saw back yards and gardens that had been hidden from view when he was looking through a car window or when he was walking. They passed the small fabrics market on the corner, lengths of bright cloth spread out between branches of trees in the shade; drove past the row of shops with a small supermarket where Amai had done much of her shopping; and continued on down another street with larger bungalows. A huge billboard loomed up on the left with a beautiful woman on it and her golden glow: "Sparkie, for a lighter skin. The cream for YOUR complexion. The one for YOU!"

And then there was St. Mungo's School. A car drew out in front of them, and the van halted just beside a knot of boys standing at the school gate. Sam's friend Gideon was among them. Sam took one hand off the strut to wave. "Hey!"

One of the boys turned and looked straight at him, and Sam saw his mouth fall open. The boy nudged Gideon, who lifted his arm to wave back, then let it drop, his face puzzled.

Sam stared over his shoulder as the van moved away. Was it possible that Gideon hadn't recognized him, and that was why he hadn't waved? Atate had brought Sam to school till he died, then Amai had driven him there in their Ford. Sometimes he walked, and that was all right, too, but not this! A wave of embarrassment washed over him. Was it because he was standing in an open van-bus like any poor country boy?

A real air-conditioned bus came humming up alongside, hiding the school from sight, and Sam quickly took his hand off the rail lest the bus crush it, it came so close. It loomed high above, even higher than the trucks on the road laden with sacks of the local farmers' mealie meal, and its windows were so dark that you could not see the people inside.

It would be better if they had been in the real bus. Sam glanced down at Aunty. She shook her head at him. "Too expensive," she mouthed, understanding his question before he'd even asked it.

The bus glided ahead, passing them.

The van juddered to a stop at a traffic light, and Sam lost his balance.

"Whoa!" The man beside him grabbed him. "Here. Change places with me." He made room for Sam to move up and stand in the front corner of the van. "Lost your smile, have you?"

Sam took a long, shuddering breath. He shook his head and, tentatively, he smiled.

"That's better." The man had a kind face, Sam thought. So what that Gideon hadn't waved! He probably just hadn't seen Sam, was all. Sam straightened his back.

He could hold on with both hands now, one strut on his left and one on his right. He spread his legs so that, when they set off again with yet more passengers, he stood steady as a rock. It was better there in the front, too; now he could see ahead as well as to the side.

"How far are you and your amai going?"

"She's not my amai," Sam answered quickly. "She's my aunt. My amai is late."

"Ah." The man whistled thinly through his teeth. "So where is your aunty taking you?"

"To Mandingwe." The traffic was thinning here on the outskirts of Blantyre town, and soon they had left the town completely, bowling along newly tarmacked road.

"Mandingwe, eh," joined in the man on the other side. "That's a fine place. There's a mission there. Is that where you're going?"

"I think so." Sam turned to look at him.

"Then you're a lucky boy."

There were no sidewalks out here as there were in town, but there were just as many people on the road, walking in single file where the tarmac abruptly met the earth. The lines of walkers broke up only when they met roadside stalls where women held out mangoes and bunches of bananas to the passers-by.

"I hear there's a hospital there, and a church. And a school," said the second man.

No school today, Sam thought. He'd got out of that! He

hadn't done any homework for a week and might well have been in trouble.

He'd never been to the country before. The road was climbing, and he could see hills ahead. The wind blew strong in his face and dried the trickle of tears on his cheeks.

4

"SAMMY!" SOMETHING JABBED THE CALF OF HIS LEG, AND he looked over his shoulder. "Come on!" His aunt was getting to her feet. "This is where we get out."

The van was slowing down. Ahead on the right was a cluster of five small wooden workshops. The van stopped at a corner near the first, where two men were sawing a tree trunk into planks outside on the hard-baked earth.

Sam squeezed through the standing passengers till he reached the tailgate. He climbed over it and jumped onto the road. A man lowered the tailgate for Aunt Mercy, and she scrambled down, too, and took the case that was handed to her. Three women, waiting at the roadside, got in, and the van drove off, trailing black fumes behind it.

Sam looked around. No other car, not even a truck or a bicycle, came past. The only sound was of the men sawing, and the rich, sweet smell of freshly cut wood drowned out all other smells. New chairs were stacked neatly at the entrance to their shop.

"*Muli bwanje.* Good morning, how are you?" Aunty called out to the carpenters.

One looked up, broke into a grin, and said something to his companion. The two of them put down the saw and came over, wiping sweaty hands on their shorts.

"*Ndili bwino, kaia inu.* I'm well if you are well," they answered in turn, nodding politely.

"*Ndili bwino, zikomo.* I'm well. Thank you. We're well," answered Aunty.

"Is this your nephew?" asked the older man.

"Yes, this is Samuel." She gave Sam a little push to move forward. He put out a hand to shake the hand that was offered.

"So have you come to live here in Mandingwe?"

"Just for a bit," answered Sam. He wasn't sure how long he would be staying.

The scent of fresh sawdust and cut wood was even stronger now that the men were standing in front of them. "We are happy to see you. Are you happy to be here?"

Sam shrugged. How could he tell?

"He is happy," Aunty stated firmly. "I notice that it is not chairs that you are making." She gestured at the wood they were working on. Now that they weren't blocking the view, Sam could see that it wasn't a chair; the pieces were longer. *A coffin.* He stared at it.

"It is not," agreed the older man. "Do you know Courage Makelele?"

"From along by the brick furnace?"

"The same."

"*Tssk.*" Aunty clicked her tongue on the roof of her mouth. There was a short, respectful silence.

How slow and simple their language was out here in the country, thought Sam, looking around. He fidgeted, wondering where they were going. There were no houses here, nor mud huts, only the small row of workshops. It didn't look much like a "fine village" to him. Not the way the man on the van had said.

They turned and set off down a track of dark red earth. It was bumpy and hollowed out in places from the rain, and trees crowded in on either side as if they wanted to crush it. Sam glanced back at the tarmacked road, the link to Blantyre town and home. The older man was standing there, right in the middle of the dirt track. Behind him it was empty.

5

AUNT MERCY DIDN'T SPEAK AS THEY SET OFF DOWN the track, not even to tell Sam how far they'd be walking. He hoped it wouldn't take long, but he could see no more signs of any village or mission and was beginning to wonder. Then, above the singing of the birds, came the *squeak, squeak* of a bicycle behind him and a rattle of wheels on the bumpy track. A teenage youth drew level with them, the smudge of a mustache above his lip.

"Hello, how are you?" asked the cyclist, putting bare feet out to the ground to brake. He dismounted.

Aunt Mercy stopped. "I'm well, if you are well."

"I'm well, thank you," he answered. "Here, let me take those for you."

Aunty hesitated, just for a moment, then handed over the case. "Pass him your bag," she said to Sam, and "Thank you, Mavuto Matola."

Sam looked carefully at the youth. He had two teeth missing in front and was wearing frayed shorts. His T-shirt said IT'S THE REAL THING but you couldn't see what was real because of all the holes and old stains. Was he trouble, as the name "Mavuto" meant? Why else would Aunt Mercy have hesitated when he offered to help carry the heavy bags?

Mavuto turned to Sam. "Are you the nephew?"

Sam nodded.

"So you'll be coming to school here, too?"

Sam glanced sideways at Aunty and nodded once more.

"Where *you* should still be, Mavuto." Aunty clicked her tongue against the roof of her mouth. "You may be fifteen years old, but you are still able to learn."

Mavuto looked abashed. Then he grinned. "If I was still at that bloody school, I would not be helping you with these."

"If you were still at school . . . if you were still at school," grumbled Aunty. "If you were at school, you would know full well that yesterday was the last day of term. And I do not wish to hear such language." She ignored the face that Mavuto pulled at her.

Sam didn't know whether to cheer or sulk when he heard that. Just earlier he'd been glad to have another day off, but that had been in Blantyre, and the school had been St. Mungo's.

He'd never even said goodbye to his classmates, apart from that wave. There hadn't been time, it had all happened so quickly. What if they forgot him? What if someone else sat at his desk—in the third row from the back, next to the window, next to Gideon—and never knew it was his place? And now he was here, and what on earth was he going to do in this bush village if they were already on holiday? Ride around on a bicycle like Mavuto and help carry suitcases?

They walked on in silence, their feet slapping up little puffs of dust from the ground. On the left the trees thinned out and looked less threatening. A small house appeared, with smooth mud walls and a thatched roof, roughly square in shape. There was another behind it, and another alongside, both of dark red brick. Sam counted six houses. And then Aunty and Mavuto turned off to the left.

The rear wheel of the bicycle bumped over the root of a tree and the bag fell off. "Bloody bag!"

"Mavuto!"

He ignored her. Four children were charging out from behind the hut. It was brick, not mud. Sam's mother had been wrong about that. "Amai! Aunty! What have you brought us?"

Aunt Mercy put an arm round Sam's shoulders and propelled him forward. "I have brought you your cousin Samuel. Sammy, this is Enock, and this is Ezelina. We sometimes call her Ezza."

Two children dressed in faded cotton shirts, one in a skirt, the other in shorts—about his own age, Sam guessed—smiled at him with faces that shone. They were his height, all right, but where he was sturdy, they were thin and wiry. They looked alike, right down to the way their eyebrows met in the middle, except for the two tiny plaits sticking out from Ezelina's head and the skirt that she was wearing. Sam noticed Enock's eyes widen as he spotted Sam's running shoes. Sam grinned at Enock.

"And this is Macdonald." Macdonald was tall, and older, with a funny scar. It was long and shiny and stretched from his left eye across his cheek and down to his top lip. Macdonald's arms dangled awkwardly at his sides, as if they didn't know where they belonged. He nodded when his name was mentioned but didn't look up. The way he went and stood next to Mavuto made Sam think they were friends. "And this"—Aunty scooped up a toddler—"is little Chikondi."

Chikondi chuckled at Sam.

"Chikondi is Ezelina and Enock's cousin. He is the son of my late husband's late sister. Macdonald is his brother. Their atate is the son of your mother's cousin."

Other children had come running now and were crowding round, staring at Sam the newcomer, who was still trying to work out in his mind where Macdonald and Chikondi fitted in.

"Take your bags from Mavuto, Sammy."

Sammy? "I'm Sam," he said indignantly.

She grunted. "Macdonald, Ezelina, Enock," she addressed the children, "I have to go to the doctors'. I'm already late. Macdonald, you show Sammy where he will sleep, and help him with his things." She gave Sam a big hug. "Go with them. They'll look after you."

She smoothed her dress, patted her hair, and went off.

Sam smiled at Macdonald but stepped back when he saw Macdonald's scowl. The next second the scowl was gone.

Could he have imagined it? Macdonald said something to Mavuto that Sam couldn't hear, then picked up Sam's case in one hand and the bag in the other and headed for the hut. Mavuto cycled slowly away.

"Is she sick?" Sam asked Ezelina, who was walking beside him.

"Who?"

"Aunty."

"Why?"

Was she deaf or something? "Because she's going to the doctor."

"Oh, no." Ezelina giggled. She put her hand over her mouth to stop any more laughter.

"The foreign doctor has a wife who's a doctor, too. Amai looks after their babies when they are working at the hospital," Enock explained.

"And the babies are twins like me and Enock," Ezelina added proudly. "I'll take you there, if you like. Amai won't let us in the doctors' house. If we do, the dog will come after us."

"And bite us."

"But we can go round the back."

Ezelina and Enock led Sam inside. It was dark and cool. Behind Sam the others crowded in the doorway to watch. He could feel their eyes on his back, and he turned. They giggled. One or two of them waved. Macdonald had dropped his suitcase at the door and was gazing outside, over the heads of the gawping children.

Sam turned back. The house, if you could call it that, was no bigger than the sitting room at home in town. It didn't have a dark blue floor or framed pictures on the wall. There was a table, but it was small and plain, not like the polished dining table at home. There were three stools around it, and a single chair. In the middle of the concrete floor was a pole. His eyes traveled up it to the tightly packed dried grass of the dome-shaped roof. He dropped his eyes. There was a screen over to one side and behind it a bed. Some cushions and rolled-up mats, three of them, lay at the foot of the bed.

Enock was at his elbow. "This is our home," he said proudly.

This was all? Sam swallowed hard. "Do you sleep here?"

"Yes, of course."

"On mats?"

"What's the matter?" Ezza looked worried. "Did you forget to bring your mat with you?"

Sam gulped. "I haven't got a mat. I sleep in a bed."

"Like Amai, you mean?" Enock stroked the bed's thin mattress.

"Sort of. It's a proper bed with a wooden headboard and footboard. They're yellow. I painted them myself, with Amai. And there's a shelf above for my books and stuff. And a light to read by."

"Oh. Well, Enock and I sleep nearest to the wall," Ezelina told him. "Chikondi sleeps with our amai."

"That's because Chikondi's only little and Amai has to be

with him," Enock broke in, perching on the edge of the bed. He scratched the scab over a sore on his arm.

"What are the bricks there for?" Sam nodded at the bricks, one under each foot of the bed, right by one of Enock's swinging legs.

"It's to protect Chikondi from the *tokoloshes*."

Sam knew about tokoloshes. Atate had said the spirits didn't like town and stayed away, but Sam's friends talked about them, and the neighbor, too, and Sam knew that if you weren't careful and respectful, they could harm you. He frowned. "But what about if you sleep on the floor?"

"What do you mean?" Enock spoke quietly.

"Well, if you have to be raised higher to be safe from tokoloshes, it must be scary to sleep on the floor." Sam's voice had dropped, too.

Enock and Ezelina looked at each other. This hadn't occurred to them.

"We're all right," said Enock.

"I think they leave mat sleepers alone," Ezelina said at the same time.

"Or maybe there isn't one here at the moment," Sam suggested.

"Mmm. Anyway"—Ezelina pointed—"Jesus is up there. He protects us."

Enock nodded in agreement.

Sam took a couple of paces and peered up at the faded picture pinned above the door. He could just make out the figure of Jesus with his hands outstretched, and he felt relieved.

"Hey! Your shoes have got lights!" Enock slipped off the bed in excitement. "Move your foot again."

Sam did so. In the darkness of the hut, you could see the little flashes.

"Does he sleep here, too?" Sam's eyes were on Macdonald's stiff back. The children outside were drifting away.

Enock nodded. "Yes, of course. Can I try them on?"

"What?"

"Your shoes."

"Where'll I sleep then?" Sam asked Ezelina, not really listening to Enock.

"Amai will decide," said Ezelina. "Maybe she'll give you Mpatso's mat; it's under the mattress."

"Who's Mpatso?" Was this another cousin? Where was he?

"He's late. He lived here till November, then he died." Enock was very matter-of-fact about it. "Go on, let me try on your shoes. Please? I want to see the lights."

"Was he your brother?" Sam asked Ezelina.

Ezelina shook her head. "No. Chikondi's brother. He didn't live with us for long."

"Oh." Perhaps they'd all die, one by one, and perhaps he'd be next—because he hadn't even started to live with them yet. Or maybe Chikondi would. He looked hard at the toddler, but Chikondi looked healthy enough to him.

Enock stopped scratching and grinned at Sam. "Will you let me try them on later?"

"And me?" Macdonald had come closer and was gazing at the lights, too.

Sam frowned. "Okay." But he didn't really think he wanted them to try his shoes on. He just wanted to stop them asking. "Where do I put my things?"

Ezelina picked up the suitcase with both hands, struggled over to the corner with it, and set it down. "In here, of course." She brushed her hand across its lid, stroking it.

Macdonald turned away and left the hut.

"I mean"—Sam was puzzled—"where should I put my clothes?"

Now it was her turn not to understand. "Put them?"

"Well, where do you put yours?"

Enock pointed at the wall. Nails were driven into it, and from them dripped a small assortment of trousers and shirts and cloths. "Ezza and I share a nail."

"And Macdonald shares one with Chikondi," Ezelina finished for him. "You can use your case. Amai's got a box under the bed."

Sam could see that there really wasn't room for a chest of drawers. Miserably, he flopped down onto his case and sighed. It was all so different, even more than he could have imagined. Through the open doorway he saw a rooster stretch and flap its wings and crow. The chickens pecking the ground ignored it.

Sam got back up. He undid the latches of his case and opened the lid.

The others crowded round.

"You've got a book!" Enock breathed. "May I see?"

"I've got two," Sam boasted, confident once more. "Here!" He passed the thinner one over, *The Travels of Mansa Musa*.

Enock wiped his hands on his shorts before taking the book. He carried it to the table and sat down, Ezelina beside him. They sat close together, turning the pages. Chikondi played at their feet.

Behind them, Sam was taking out his parents' wedding photograph in its heavy frame. He looked round the room for a place to put it. On one wall was a small cupboard—just two shelves, really—behind a thin cotton curtain. On top was a glass and a bowl. He stretched up and rested the photograph beside the bowl, then stepped back. There. Now he could see his amai and atate, and they could see him.

Suddenly, he felt an overwhelming urge to get out of the small dark hut and be in the open. He stood over the twins and waited till they looked up at him. He took his book away from them, put it back in his case, and closed the case. They were so surprised, they didn't protest

He went outside and leaned against the hot brick wall. Macdonald was over at the edge of the track, sitting on a sticking-up tree root, staring into space. Just then, a big four-by-four swung into view, bumping down the track, with a tail of boys and girls running behind, calling out and laughing. Enock raced out to join them. Macdonald didn't budge. Sam's legs twitched, and he began jogging toward it, too. It was a Toyota, like Gideon's father's. A foreigner was at the wheel, a white man with fair hair sticking up in clumps. Sam waved to him. But when the man didn't acknowledge him or any of them, Sam dropped back, and Enock and the others ran on without him.

6

"Is Enock coming back?"

"Sure. When he feels like it." Ezelina tossed her head. "Me and Macdonald are going for bananas. Do you want to come?"

"Yes," said Sam. Maybe there'd be a shop. It would be good to see a shop, have a look round, see what they sold.

Macdonald scowled.

Ezelina scooped Chikondi off the ground. She leaned forward at the waist, hoisted him onto her back, and tied him on with her cloth.

"Are we going to the doctors' house, too?" Sam asked. He wanted to see Aunt Mercy again. "You said we could."

"After we've got the bananas."

The three of them came to a small market. Mostly it was women sitting behind cloths spread on the ground, with fruit and vegetables. There were a few rickety tables up on thin legs, just three, with leafy roofs for shelter. Tiny fish were piled in an untidy gray heap on one of them, and potatoes and tomatoes were arranged in small pyramids on another. On the third table lay a row of wooden skewers with mice neatly impaled on them, gray wiry tails hanging down over the edge.

"I wish you a good day," said Ezelina to a woman seated on the ground with six bunches of bananas spread out on her cloth.

"I've accepted your wish," said the woman. "How are you?"

"I am well if you are well."

"I am well, *zikomo*, thank you. Have you come for bananas?"

"Yes, Aunty."

There would be no shop, Sam realized, looking round, pulling a face. This was it.

He trudged over to Macdonald, who had his back to the market and was watching boys playing soccer. Behind a wide open space with goalposts was a long, low building, with another at right angles.

"What's that?" Sam pointed.

"School." Macdonald didn't turn.

Sam narrowed his eyes, examining the long building. The open windows of the mission school stared blankly at him. There was a gaggle of girls on the verandah, fooling around. He looked back at the soccer.

"St. Mungo's is bigger," he said. "I go there by car in the morning. That's my school—St. Mungo's," he explained. He bit his lip as he saw the odd expression on Macdonald's face. "This one looks all right, too," he said quickly.

Macdonald grunted and ran off just as Ezelina and Chikondi came up to them.

"I like soccer," Sam told Ezelina wistfully, looking after Macdonald.

"You can play if you want," she said. "Macdonald!" she shouted, but Macdonald didn't answer. He was busy calling out to the others as he ran.

Sam fidgeted. He was only trying to tell them how he lived at home.

"Go on, then." Ezelina nudged him.

He badly wanted to join in, but it would be difficult just going over, especially with Macdonald being the way he was. Macdonald hadn't even asked if he wanted to play, even though at St. Mungo's Sam had been on the team. But maybe Macdonald hadn't asked because he was older.

"It's all right, I'll stay with you." But tomorrow he'd play for sure.

"As you like."

He thought Ezelina sounded annoyed. Nothing he said seemed to be right. But then she grinned at him. "Come on, let's go to Amai." On her back Chikondi seemed to have fallen asleep. His eyes were closed, and his head lolled to one side. There was a small smile on his lips.

They went on up past the school, past four neat brick bungalows on their left, then a church. "Our atate helped build that when he was our age," Ezelina told him proudly, pointing at a square building. "That's the children's ward. It's where the children sleep who have to come to hospital."

"Oh. Where is your father?"

"He's late. Like yours, and your mother. He's buried down there." She pointed down a path.

Sam stumbled over a large stone, half-buried in a rut, and just managed to save himself from falling. Ezelina was going off to the side, to a large bungalow with wicker chairs scattered on a verandah. Sam stopped. It looked so familiar. He spotted the Toyota, parked now under the trees. The only car he'd seen since he arrived.

A black dog barked from the verandah, making Sam jump. It bounded down the steps toward them. He ducked behind Ezelina.

"It's all right," she said, a bit shrilly. "Just stay quite still."

"It'll bite us." Sam was trembling. "Enock said so."

"It won't. Not if we stay outside the house."

He tried to stand as still as Ezelina. The dog came up to his waist. It sniffed him and pushed its wet nose at his hand. Sam shrank back. It gave a little jump at Ezelina.

"Just come." But her voice quavered.

Sam followed Ezelina, and the dog followed Sam, so closely that he could feel its hot breath. When they got to the corner of the house, the hot breath seemed to stop. Sam chanced a look back. The dog was panting, watching them. Then it flopped on the ground, lifted a leg, and began licking itself.

Around another corner and they were at the back. There was Aunty on the concrete floor outside the kitchen with two plump babies on a rush mat, who looked as pleased to see Sam and Ezelina and Chikondi as Aunt Mercy did.

The beating of Sam's heart slowed.

"Sammy! Hello. Come and meet the boys."

Ezelina untied Chikondi and put him down. He crawled at once toward Aunt Mercy.

"This one is Robbie, and that one is Bart," Aunty said.

Sam squatted down to their level and held out a finger, which Robbie grabbed. They had fine, straight hair, the color of a ripe peeled banana, thought Sam, and big blue eyes that were turned gravely on him till Robbie broke into gurgling laughter and Bart pushed a red toy truck over toward Sam.

And Sam started to cry. At first he hardly noticed that he was crying, the tears sprang silently from his eyes and had nothing to do with his mind, they just came. The dog that had come bounding at them. The way everything was so new and strange. Sam didn't know what he was doing here at this bungalow, so like home, but home was gone, and he wasn't in a bungalow now with rooms and a kitchen like this one; he was supposed to live in a small hut with no electricity and no room to himself, not even a bed, and lots of others to share with, and no shops to go to and no car to go in.

Bart pushed the red truck into Sam's arms, waiting for him to stop crying, and when he didn't, opened his mouth and started howling. The minute Robbie heard his brother cry, he joined in. Chikondi frowned, puzzled, then opened his mouth and began crying, too, to keep the others company.

"Oh, my." Aunt Mercy picked up Bart and cuddled him. "There, now." She hushed Robbie, while Ezelina hushed Chikondi. Aunt Mercy held out a hand to Sam. "There now," she said to him, too. From a low table at her side she took a plastic saucer and passed it over. There were chunks of avocado on it. "Take some, and pass it to Ezza."

There was no spoon or fork on the saucer, and the first piece Sam picked up slithered from his grasp. He reached out for an avocado chunk again, more carefully this time, and succeeded in getting it to his mouth. He closed his eyes as he squashed the soft green fruit against the roof of his mouth and thought of Amai lying in bed those last days, looking out of the window up at the leaves of the mango tree. In his mind, Amai smiled sweetly at him as he squashed the smooth fruit with his tongue and swallowed it. He hiccupped, wiped his nose on the back of his hand, and sniffed hard.

"Leave Chikondi and the bananas with me," Aunt Mercy said, "and go off and fetch the firewood for tonight's supper. Here," she added. "Take two." She broke off two bananas and gave them to Ezelina. Sam eyed them hungrily. Aunt Mercy and he had eaten rice and egg at breakfast time, but nothing since. That was a long time ago—and so very far away.

SAM HELD HIS BREATH AS THEY ROUNDED THE DOCTORS'
bungalow again, and dared to glance up at the verandah. The
dog's head appeared. Its eyes looked out at him, and there
was the sound of a tail beating the wooden floor, but the dog
didn't get up. Sam relaxed.

Something crashed above their heads, and he jumped, his
heart thudding once more.

Ezelina giggled. Something bumped and tumbled down
the roof. "Watch to see where it lands."

"What lands?"

"The avocado," she answered, concentrating.

There was a thump as the fruit hit the ground, and
Ezelina was there before him. She held up the avocado tri-
umphantly. "It's the monkeys," she said, "up there," pointing up into the trees. "They pick them and throw them at the
house. We'll take this one."

When they came out on the dirt track, Mavuto was there
on his bicycle, cycling round and round in circles, hands on
hips, whistling under his breath.

"Hey, Ezza! Sam!" He lost his balance as he caught sight
of them, and the bicycle bumped down hard on a hollow in
the earth and almost tipped over. "Bloody bike!" he cursed,

putting out a foot to save himself. "You coming for a ride?" he asked Sam.

"I don't think he is," Ezelina answered for him, biting her lip.

"Oh, come on, Ezza. I'll bring him back safe and sound."

"No." This time she sounded firmer. "We have to go to fetch wood. I'm showing him."

"Showing him, are you!" He leaned over and pulled one of her plaits.

"Ow! That hurt!" She lifted her hand to her head.

"Hey, what's in your hand?"

She showed him the avocado.

"From there?" He pointed. She nodded.

"Give it here." He lunged for it.

"That's mine! Give it back!"

"It isn't yours. You stole it."

"Didn't."

"Did. Anyway, look, you've got bananas in your other hand. And I'm hungry."

"Oh, all right, then. Take it."

Mavuto flung down his bicycle, dug his nails into the fruit, and began peeling it and sucking the green flesh.

"Down here." Ezelina quickly nudged Sam away. "Watch out!" as he nearly tripped over the same stone as before. "He's always hungry, Mavuto," she said as Sam heard the squeak of Mavuto's pedals cycling away from them.

They passed the side of the hospital wards, each one low, long, and white. Grass grew in between the wards, and there were bushes of flowers, roses and hibiscus. At the front there was a free-standing arch, with a sign hanging from it. On it was painted, in the same green paint as the wards' window frames, ST. ANDREW'S MISSION HOSPITAL. Outside the hospital and on the other side of the track, the grassy slope was dotted with patients, some in the shade of the trees, some in the sun. There was chatter and coughing and the cry of a child. Others sat quietly, listlessly. Sam remembered that listless look. Amai had had it, and Atate, and the people in the hospital waiting to see the doctor.

Ezelina seemed to be scanning the groups, looking for someone. "There!" she said. "Come." She beckoned him up the grassy slope on the left, past clothing hanging on lines and bushes to dry. They picked their way among the seated groups and stopped at a respectful distance from a man sitting on his own.

"*Muli bwanje*. Hello, how are you?" she said.

"*Ndilo bwino, kaia inu*." The man looked at her and smiled. "I'm well if you are well." His face was thin and drawn. His body, too, was lean and bony.

"*Ndilo bwino, zikomo*. I'm well, thank you," answered Ezelina.

The man squinted up at Sam through milky-looking eyes. "And who is this young man?"

"This is Sammy, Uncle. The Lord has taken his father

and his mother. He is my cousin, and he has come to live with us."

"Ah." The man kept his silence for a moment, peering up at Sam. "My condolences. Well, now, Sammy, I know your name, so you should know mine. They call me Brown. *Muli bwanje.*"

"*Ndilo bwino, kaia inu,*" Sam responded, trying hard not to stare. The man had one arm shorter than the other. His right arm had been cut off at the elbow.

"Sit, sit," said Brown, when the greeting was finished.

They flopped down beside him.

Ezelina reached out and touched Brown's short arm.

He smiled at her. "It is good that I am here, is it not? Well, young Sammy, do you not wish to touch me, too?"

Sam swallowed. He'd never been so close to anyone who was one-legged or one-armed or one-eyed or one-anythinged before. He'd never yet touched anyone who wasn't symmetrical. Doing that was lucky, the neighbor in town had told him. His father had scoffed. Ignorant superstition, he'd said, it was the old way, the country way, and Sam shouldn't listen. But Atate was dead, and Sam was here.

Brown moved his stumpy arm toward Sam. Sam touched.

"There, now. Your day will be a good one, will it not?" Brown smiled at them again. "You must keep coming to see me, young Sammy, like your cousin here. Then I will have company, and you will have good fortune, praise the Lord."

"Where is your guardian?" Ezelina frowned. Like every-one at the hospital, Brown had someone from his family to care for him, and cook and wash.

He turned and called, "Stella!"

A plump woman with her hair tied away under a cotton doekie emerged from the laundry house behind him, drops of water on her ankles making them sparkle in the sunshine. "What is it, old man? I'm still busy with your washing."

"She is Stella," he said to Sam as the woman went back inside. Sam could hear the splashing of water and voices raised. He liked this hospital, he thought with a little jerk of surprise, and he liked this place, like an outside waiting room. *Why couldn't Amai have been here?*

"My daughter is a good woman, and she takes care of me. Like your aunt, Sammy. Mercy is a good woman, too. We played together when we were your age." He sighed. "Off you go now. Fetch that wood!"

Sam blinked. How did he know they were off for wood?

Brown smiled at him. "This is the way Ezelina always takes for wood," he said. "There is no mystery."

"It is the way I shall take, too," said Sam gravely, getting to his feet as they said their goodbyes.

They set off down the track, past the old woman with her pyramid of drink cans for sale, past the child selling peanuts, the woman frying banana fritters over a cooking fire, the sugar cane for chewing leaning on the verge waiting to be bought, and another boy with a plate of homemade sweets.

Sam stopped at a table with bunches of herbs and saucers with crushed-up twigs on them. He peered at a jar with something coiled and brown inside. He reached out to pick it up for a better look.

"Don't!" Ezelina knocked his hand away. "He's the *sing'anga,*" she whispered, looking respectfully at the man behind the table. He was staring at a spot somewhere above their heads, ignoring them.

"Oh." Sam drew in his breath. He hadn't actually ever seen a sing'anga before, and had never expected that one would wear ordinary trousers and a white shirt. One day he'd come home and Amai's friend had been there pleading: "You could at leatht try the thing'anga'th medithine." "How could that help?" Amai had said. "I haven't long," and they had broken off as he came into the room. The friend had left a bottle at the bedside when she left. "Try it." And Amai had. "Ugh! Throw it away!" she'd told Sam. "It's disgusting!"

He hadn't. He had taken it out into the garden. There he had dug a hole under her favorite bush, a yellow mimosa. He stood the bottle upright in the hole so that the medicine was safe, and as he covered it lightly with soil, he had prayed, "O mighty spirit in the bottle, please send out your rays to her and get her better." Then he had cut some of the yellow flow- ering twigs and put them in water in a jam jar and set them beside her bed. Every time just before they wilted, he had cut more, taking away the dead ones only after putting the new ones there, so that there were always some live mimosa twigs beside her. It had worked, a bit. The doctors had given Amai four weeks, but it was ten before she went. Sam had counted.

He looked back over his shoulder at the man as they passed, but the man was staring impassively ahead.

Sam whirled and ran back. "Please . . ."

The sing'anga looked down at him.

"*Muli bwanje,*" Sam said quickly.

"*Ndili bwino, kaia inu.*" The man's voice was so deep, it could have come up from the ground beneath his feet.

"*Ndili bwino, zikomo.* Please, if Amai had taken sing'anga medicine, would she still be alive?"

"Child, I do not know your amai."

What kind of answer was that? "Tell me!" Sam almost stamped his foot, except that Ezelina was there, tugging at his arm.

"Come on, Sam." She pulled him away.

"What's the matter?" he protested. "Are you scared of him or something?" He craned his head back to look.

She still had his arm in an iron grip. "No. He's just a medicine man."

"Why, then?"

"You're so cheeky!"

"But he wouldn't answer." Sam looked back again. The man was staring into space. It was as if they'd never spoken. "I put sing'anga medicine in the ground when Amai wouldn't take it," and he told her about it in a rush.

"My atate had sing'anga herbs. But he was probably

meant to die," she said matter-of-factly. "Maybe you should have asked the *nchimi* for a spell."

He stood stock-still. A shiver wriggled up his spine. Atate and Amai had said that witch doctors no longer had power, but Gideon had laughed at him when he'd told him that and had said that they were good and strong all right in the bush.

"Have you ever done that?"

"Of course not."

"Not when your atate was ill?"

She shook her head.

"Is there one here, nearby?" The words came tumbling out.

She shook her head, nodded, looked anxious.

"Are you scared of the nchimi?"

She faced him, looking very serious. "Ask about the nchimi and you'll be turned into a cockroach."

"A cockroach!" Sam was horrified. Then someone would stamp on him and crunch and squelch him dead. He stood there, imagining it.

Ezelina wasn't waiting. She was already round the corner.

Sam sighed. It was all too late anyway. Amai was gone.

When he caught up with Ezelina, there was no sun anymore and no grass, only shade from the trees growing high on either side of the track, and chickens scratching the ground.

They passed a shack with bags of flour and sugar and tins

of dried milk arranged on the windowsill for sale. Two bunches of bananas were placed beneath on an upturned crate. Sam's mouth began to water. He wished they could stop and have the bananas Aunty had given them.

"Here is a good place," said Ezelina, when they were halfway up the edge of a field, under an old tree. "Pick as many sticks as you can carry."

"We don't need wood at home," he said to her back as she bent to gather wood. "We cook on an electric stove."

She grunted.

He sighed, then he bent, too, and they gathered the wood in silence. When they stopped, her pile was bigger than his, and she had to straighten his untidy one till the sticks were laid neatly end to end like hers. "Hold them still." She added them to her collection, took a frayed bit of string from her pocket, and tied them up. She hoisted them up onto her head and set off again.

She turned round when she realized that he wasn't following. "What are you doing?"

Sam had a stick in his hand and was cleaning one of his blue shoes. He pushed out his left foot. "My shoes. Look, they're dirty. Amai will be cross." He dropped his head so he wouldn't catch Ezelina's eye. His amai wasn't there anymore. Well, then, Aunty would be cross. "She gave them to me for my birthday."

"Why are you wearing them if they're special? If you don't wear them, they won't get dirty, will they?" Ezelina called over her shoulder as she went back toward the track. She didn't seem to care. But wearing them now made Sam feel that Amai was nearer. Besides, they showed that he wasn't just a village boy.

"Amai," he whispered. "Amai." He wished he was with her again at his real home in the town. He'd felt all right seeing the hospital, meeting Brown, gathering firewood. But this wasn't home. Only people out here in the bush bought medicine from the sing'anga as well as from the doctor. But he had touched Brown's stump, hadn't he, and he'd never thrown away his amai's medicine. So what did that make him? He had smart blue running shoes because his family wasn't poor, they weren't ignorant; only people in the bush and poor people went without shoes. That's what Amai always said. Aunt Mercy had been wearing shoes. Ezelina hadn't, nor any of his cousins when he'd arrived, though Ezelina was wearing rubber flip-flops now.

All the same, he liked her, even if she was poor and ignorant. "Wait for me!"

When he caught up with her at the side of the track, she lifted the pile of firewood off her head and laid it carefully on the earth. "We'll have our bananas." She perched on a stone at the side of the road and spread out her skirt. Sam took the one she passed him, and they peeled and ate them and sat in silence, munching. Sam closed his eyes. Suddenly, he was tired, so tired he could fold himself up on the ground here and go to sleep.

Just as his head drooped, Ezelina nudged him. "See where the sun is?" She squinted up at the sky. "We have to take the wood home."

The sun was lower now, coming close to the side of the mountain that took up half the sky ahead of them.

"Is it dangerous?" Sam squinted up there, too.

"Mount Mandingwe?"

"Is it?" he asked again.

"Strangers climb it sometimes, strangers from other countries, foreigners. There are villages up there, I think." She frowned. "It's over there, and we are over here. It will not move to come and get us, and we do not walk on its slopes. If we did, we'd be turned into lizards."

"Says who?"

"Says everyone."

"But you've just said strangers go up it."

She shrugged. "Strangers are different. Anyway, it guards us. See?" She got to her feet and spun round. "Wherever we are, we can see it, and wherever we are, it watches us."

The mountain stood alone, high above the bushes and grass and earth, its top shrouded in cloud, so that Sam couldn't see how high it reached. He imagined a huge pair of eyes inside the cloud and dropped his eyes quickly.

"It's like my atate's spirit," she said.

"And my amai's," he said stoutly.

8

WHEN SAM WOKE UP, FOR A MOMENT HE DIDN'T KNOW where he was.

He turned on his back and winced. The floor beneath him was chilly. This wasn't his bed at home. He was lying on a mat on hard, cold concrete.

A shutter over the window was tightly fastened, but a chink of light was just creeping across the floor from a small crack at the side of the closed door. He rolled his head to the side. Bravely, he dared himself to peer into the darkness underneath the bed. No tokolosh. He breathed out in relief. At least, no tokolosh that he could see.

On the bed was Aunty, with Chikondi curled up safely against her. Sam rolled his head to the other side. In a row next to him, each on a mat, were Macdonald and then Enock. Ezelina was next to Enock. Everyone was sleeping.

Sam stared up into the roof. There was a rustling up there in the branches as a lizard scuttled across.

As he looked down, he caught movement to his right. Macdonald's eyes were open and examining him. Their eyes locked. The night before, when Sam had come back from the outside latrine, he had found Macdonald looking in his case, and the others watching. He hadn't known what to say and had just stood there watching, too, as Macdonald rifled through his things. He wouldn't have minded if Macdonald had asked. Or, at least, he wouldn't have minded as much. And Macdonald had seemed to be taunting him by going on with him there. A minute later he'd stopped and closed the lid. No words had been spoken.

Now Macdonald turned his back on Sam.

Sam closed his eyes and drifted back into uneasy sleep. In his dream Brown was hobbling toward him on a crutch, holding out his stumpy arm. "Kiss it," Brown ordered. Tall, skinny Macdonald was standing between them, laughing. His laughter became a cackling, and Macdonald came closer and closer till he was cackling in Sam's face and there were flames behind him and black smoke billowing and the scar on his cheek was tight and shiny, and Sam saw that it was a burn scar.

When Sam woke again, the shutter had been pulled back and light was pouring into the hut. Enock was rolling up his mat, and in the doorway the cock was standing high on its feet, flapping its wings and crowing to the world.

For a moment Sam's heart lifted. Then the dream rushed back into his mind, and he felt strange again. He used to ask his mother why he didn't have brothers and sisters. He'd wanted to be part of a bigger family. Now he wished he was on his own again, and at home, with Amai.

Ezelina was over by the wall, wearing homemade knickers. She took a skirt and a shirt down from the nail, shook them, and began pulling them on. Sam quickly shut his eyes as he saw Aunt Mercy approach. She leaned over him.

"Good morning, precious." She hugged him.

Over her shoulder, Sam saw Macdonald watching them, a hungry look on his face. Sam looked away quickly.

"Go and wash at the tap." His aunt tilted his face and rubbed his cheek with her thumb. "Go on, now. The others are all up and dressed. At first everything will feel odd and different. Breakfast will help."

The evening before had passed in a blur, he'd been so tired. He vaguely remembered Aunt Mercy coming home and cooking; then, soon after the meal, he'd unrolled his mat when he was told to, and lain down.

Outside now, Aunt Mercy squatted at the fire and stirred something in a pan, Chikondi at her side on the ground, grinning and gurgling. Macdonald and a couple of other boys were playing with sticks and a stone, but from where Sam was he couldn't make out what the game was.

He went out to the tap that stood at the side of the yard, splashed water on his face and neck, and rubbed hard. Mud squelched up between his toes from where water had dripped before and made the earth wet. He didn't like it and went back inside to put on his shoes but didn't get a chance.

"You need to roll up your mat or my amai'll be cross." Ezelina was taking bowls from the shelf and putting them on the table.

"What are you doing?" Enock asked her. "Why are we eating in here?"

"It's to make him feel at home," Ezelina answered quietly. "Just for today. Amai says he ate inside in town, see."

Sam felt hot and silly. It was him they were talking about. The meal last night had been outside, but he'd barely noticed it, had wanted nothing more than to lie down and escape into sleep.

"Chase it!" Enock shouted. "Tumbu fly! Kill it!"

"Where?"

"There!"

Sam biffed the insect with his shoe. It twitched, lay still. Enock immediately started scratching his elbow.

"Don't scratch!" Ezelina scolded. "Tumbu," she explained to Sam.

He nodded. If they landed on your clothes, they laid eggs that hatched under your skin. Unless Amai was there to iron the clothes really well. That killed the eggs.

Enock scrunched up his nose at his bossy twin.

"Will you fill this bowl for me from the tap outside?" Ezelina asked Sam.

When he gave the plastic bowl back to her, carefully and without spilling a drop, she handed it round for them to rinse their hands. Aunt Mercy sat on the chair, Macdonald on one stool, Enock on another. "Let Sam have the third stool," Aunt Mercy told Ezelina. Ezelina's face showed no expression. She took her place at the table beside him, standing.

Sam looked at the enamel plate in front of him. It was yellow with a pink rim. He glanced at Ezelina's. They were exactly the same as the ones at home.

"I took some small things," Aunt Mercy said. "I didn't think Mr. Gunya needed plates. He would only have sold them. Or taken them for himself, I shouldn't wonder."

Sam clutched his plate harder. "Let me fill it, Sam," Aunty said. He passed it over and watched her shake out a dollop of white *nsima* on it, adding a few cooked beans as relish.

He pulled the plate closer to start eating.

"We haven't said grace yet, Sammy," Aunty Mercy chided. The others stared at him.

His hands dropped to his lap.

"Good Lord, thank you today for our food and for bringing Samuel to us," said Aunty.

"Amen," they chorused.

Sam looked for a spoon on the table, but there was none, so he copied the way the others took a plug of the nsima, rolled a couple of beans into it, and carried that to their mouths. Lips smacked and mouths slurped as they rolled the thick, white, solid maize porridge with the cooked beans and ate it. Sam gripped the plate tightly with his left hand, and every time he took up a mouthful, he imagined his mother. . . . It wasn't so hard, especially as they ate in silence, as was the custom. He didn't look at anyone, just down at his plate and at the scrubbed wood of the table.

"Enock, it's your turn to fetch the firewood today. And stop scratching your arm! Sammy, you sweep the yard. Macdonald . . ." Their plates were empty, and Aunt Mercy was sharing out the tasks.

Sam stood outside with the broom that Enock passed to him, a long bunch of sticks tied in the middle. He pushed it awkwardly in front of him, pulled it back. It felt stiff, wrong. He pushed again.

"Like this," Macdonald said scornfully, elbowing him aside and taking the broom. He made semicircles in the earth around himself, turning his body easily.

"Women's work," muttered Sam.

Macdonald stopped. "Who're you calling a woman?"

Sam shrugged. "Me? No one."

"Macdonald's a woman! Macdonald's a woman!" Enock jigged gleefully.

Macdonald shoved the broom at Sam and stalked back to the tap, where he had been washing the plates.

Sam boiled inside. He'd show Macdonald. He bent for the broom, grasped it in both hands, and began to make the wide sweeping arcs as he turned. In time, his body got into the rhythm of it and he made patterns in the yard as he went, circles and half-circles and smaller arcs round the little strip of carefully tended bright red geraniums, big arcs in the emptier area, till finally the whole yard was a pattern of arcs. He surveyed it proudly. "Shoo!" he shouted at the chickens. "Go away!"—as their spindly feet made tracks on the newly brushed red earth.

One of the boys who'd been around the day before came running past, rolling an old tire in front him with a stick. When he saw Sam, he stopped. "Hey, you, Sammy!" The tire wobbled and fell over. "You like soccer?"

"I play on the school team."

"Nice one. Then come and play. Enock, you coming?" the boy called.

"He's got to finish in here," Ezelina called from inside the hut.

"Later, Ezza," Enock said. "Macdonald, coming?"

Ezelina came out. "But you haven't finished . . ."

"I have," said Sam. "Look," and he escaped inside. His running shoes were stained from the day before and a bit damp, but you could still see that they were blue. He sat on the floor and pushed his feet into them, fastened them firmly, and kicked his feet. The lights were still working.

He ran after the others. Enock made way for him, and other boys joined them as they went up the track. Macdonald and Sam were the tallest by far, but then Macdonald was a couple of years older. And Macdonald seemed to be talking about him to one of the other boys, Sam noticed uneasily, and they were laughing.

But he forgot that as soon as they were running onto the field, which wasn't a bad one, he had to admit. All right, it sloped a bit toward one goalpost at the end where the small market was, and there was hardly any grass in the goal areas. Apart from that, it was all right.

Sam soon lost himself in the game. This he knew about. He tackled and got possession and went hurtling up the field.

"Blue shoes! Here, blue shoes! To me!"

He glanced round. A boy was coming up fast on the flank, gesturing.

"Blue shoes!" shouted another boy, from the opposite team.

Sam stopped, hesitated.

"Blue shoes!" came from somewhere behind him, and Sam's opponent came barreling into him. The boy hooked a foot round and got the ball and was running off with it. Barefoot.

Sam looked round. He'd never tried playing barefoot, he'd never had to. When they shouted "Blue shoes!" it had sounded mocking. He hadn't expected that. He dithered out there on the wing as the game carried on without him. Most of the boys were playing barefoot. Some wore shoes, but theirs were old and shabby, or else they wore sneakers, mostly without laces. Sam had sneakers in his case, but he couldn't go for them, not now that the game had started.

Quickly, he went behind the goal and took off his shoes, then ran back onto the field. Now he was like the others.

"Hey!" Enock said, stopping beside him and pointing down.

"I took them off. So?"

"Can I wear them, then?"

But Sam never answered him because suddenly the ball was there and they were busy keeping it away from the goal. And yes, it was uncomfortable to play barefoot when he wasn't used to it—there were little sharp stones dotted about in the grass—but he gritted his teeth and got on with it. If they could play barefoot, so could he. He would get used to it, he was determined to, he'd show them. After all, he'd been on St. Mungo's team the time they'd beaten the Mbale Under-13s.

At the end of the game, pleased with how it had gone, he ran to reclaim his shoes.

They weren't there.

"Enock!" he shouted, looking for him on the field. But he saw quickly that Enock wasn't wearing them.

He whirled round. "Where are my shoes?" he cried to the goalie.

The goalie was startled. "I don't know. Maybe someone borrowed them."

"Borrowed?" Sam was shouting now. "Thieved, you mean!"

The boys around stared, shocked.

Enock came running. "Sam is my cousin!" he cried. "Who's taken his shoes? They are fine ones. They've even got lights on." He stamped his foot.

"Yeah, and don't we know it."

Enock ignored Macdonald's comment. "Help us look," he appealed to the players.

Everyone was shouting now, everyone seemed to have something to say.

"No, come on! Let's get on with the game!"

"Who's the stranger?"

"Who's he calling a thief?"

Some did help to look but got bored when they didn't find the shoes at once. Eventually, they broke up into groups and sloped off.

Sam ran to the foreign doctors' house, just as he had used to run to Amai. At the hedge he hesitated. Then he ran his fastest round the corner. The dog barked and he heard its paws pad down the verandah, but he'd managed to surprise it and he was faster. "My shoes!" he shouted, as he rounded the corner to the back. "Someone's stolen them. Amai gave them to me for my birthday!"

"Quiet now, or you will get the babies going," said Aunty. "Shh, shh. Tell me what happened."

But when he had finished blurting out the story to her, she didn't draw him to her. Not the way Amai would have done.

"Why did you leave them there, you daft monkey?"

As if it was his fault! He stared at her.

"What were you doing wearing them for soccer anyway? You have a perfectly good pair of gym shoes. I saw you pack them."

"Because . . ." He stared at the ground. *Because I wanted to show them off,* he wanted to admit but didn't. Aunty might not think that was such a good reason.

"Go on home," she said. "Go on. I shall be back later."

So he left her. What else could he do? His feet were sore. At the front corner of the bungalow he made a dash for the safety of the track outside. Behind him the dog barked once, twice, but that was all; it didn't chase him.

9

BACK ON THE TRACK, SAM STUMBLED AND FELL OVER THE same stone as before. As he got up, he thought he imagined a sort of groan. But there was nothing there—at least, not that he could see. He shivered, though he wasn't cold. It was as if the stone had put itself there deliberately, he thought. He closed his eyes, trying hard to remember Atate, to see his face, to hear him saying, "It's only a stone and you're in a strange place." But he couldn't see Atate's face in his mind— and Atate was dead. "Please let me pass, stone," he said aloud. Maybe there was a tokolosh in it.

A goat bleated. It wandered through the entrance arch to the hospital, straggly tail wagging. A woman, one who was not dressed as a nurse, walked through, too. Sam hesitated, then followed, skirting the stone, a pulse in his throat beating hard in relief. The goat jumped up on the nearest verandah, and so did Sam. The goat skipped through the nearest open door, and Sam heard it bleating again. He glanced in. The goat was going from bed to bed and sniffing at the women it found lying there as if it was looking for someone. At one bed a guardian was helping a nurse to raise the patient to a sitting position.

Sam drew back. He walked along the verandah, trailing

his fingers along the wall, enjoying its roughness on his fingertips, liking the warmth of the floor on the bare soles of his feet. "You've got shoes, you don't need to go barefoot," Amai used to say. But Sam actually liked the scratchy feel of the floor underfoot. Even so, he wanted his shoes back.

A muffled curse. It came from the open window just ahead.

Sam went to it and looked in.

A square of light, and a keyboard. A computer! Modern light glowing from a modern screen. A man was banging his hands on the desk in frustration.

"*Muli bwanje!*" Sam called out from the doorway, forgetting his fear and misery in a flash.

"*Ndili bwino, kaia inu,*" came the answer as the man turned in his chair to look at Sam.

"*Ndili bwino, zikomo.*"

"Who are you?"

"I'm Sam. I've got one of those." He pointed at the computer.

The man glanced at the computer screen and back at Sam in amazement. "What, here in the village? Only the senior staff have electricity, from the generator. Have you come to stay with one of them? I don't recognize you."

"I couldn't bring it with me," Sam admitted. "I'm staying with my aunt, see. But at home I spend all day on it," he exaggerated grandly. "I'm good at computers."

"Hmm," grunted the man.

"Can I help?" Sam was in the room, without being invited.

"I doubt it." The man sighed. "This all needs to be smaller, and it's supposed to be in columns."

Sam leaned over the man's shoulder. "The whole document?" He pressed keys, and the writing and figures on the screen rearranged themselves. "Is that any good?"

"Well, yes," the man said grudgingly. "Oh, look, come on. Now show me how to put these files into a folder. Since you're here anyway."

"Easy-peasy." Sam was already pulling up a chair and sitting down. "What name do you want for the folder? Which files do you want me to put into it?"

The inner door opened. "Do you know what happened to the last delivery of syringes, Mr. Bwinji?" A tall white man stood there. He had piercing blue eyes and short fair hair, and there were dark circles under his eyes. "Hello, who are you?" he asked tiredly.

Sam pushed back his chair and got to his feet, recognizing the man from the four-by-four. So this was the foreigner Aunt Mercy worked for, Bart and Robbie's father. *"Muli bwanje."*

The man returned the greeting but abruptly.

"My name is Samuel Sangala. My amai is late, and my atate, too. And I have come to stay with my aunt, just for a little while."

The white man regarded him. He drew his arm across his

forehead to wipe off the sweat and gave a tired smile. "Thank you for explaining that. What I meant, though, was what are you doing in this office?"

"I'm helping Mr.—um, Mr. Bwinji."

"I see." He turned to Mr. Bwinji. "Is he?"

"The boy has helped me with something complicated."

Sam almost said that it hadn't been at all complicated, but he shut his mouth before the words could spring out.

"Hmm." But the man didn't sound all that happy about it, and he looked harassed. "We'll discuss this further, Mr. Bwinji—and we do need to find out where those syringes have got to. I'll be in my office." He left the room, closing the door with a firm click.

Sam sat back in the chair and rested his hands ready in front of the keyboard. "What else can I help you with? I helped Amai at her work when she was too busy." *Or too tired from the Disease.* But he didn't say that. "You haven't got any page numbers in. Don't you want them?"

"Yes, I do." Mr. Bwinji sighed. "And the font isn't right, and there are other things, too. But now please leave, because I have to go to the director's office."

"The man who just came in? Is he the doctor, too?"

"Yes, one of them. He's from Denmark."

"Oh. Where's Denmark?" Sam was playing for time.

"Up in the north of Europe."

"Why—?"

"But perhaps you can come back and help me," Mr.

Bwinji interrupted before Sam could ask any more questions.

Sam brightened. "When? Tomorrow?"

"We'll see. I'm not making any promises."

Sam jumped down from the verandah. "Ouch!" He had landed on a sharp stone.

He dawdled to the track and went back to Aunty's, as she'd told him. Now his feet seemed to land on every single sharp stone that lay in the way, and by the time he got back, he was trying not to limp.

"Someone stole my shoes," he told Ezelina. He waited for her sympathy.

He didn't get it. "You're daft. Why did you take them off?"

He glared at her. Nobody cared. He wouldn't talk about his shoes anymore, not to anyone! Anyway, maybe, he thought then, maybe if he kept quiet, they would turn up.

Amai would have cared. He went into the hut and stared at the photograph. With his finger he touched her face, very gently. Then he sat on the floor, brushed his feet clean of dust, and slipped on his sneakers. He knelt by his case, turned the key, and flung open the lid, then pushed aside his T-shirts and took out the two books that lay there. He hugged them to him.

Oliver Twist. At bedtime at home he'd climb into bed in his own room and nestle down under the sheet, and Amai would come and sit beside him, resting against the wall, her legs stretched out alongside his, and she'd read to him. On the evening of his birthday she'd asked him why he hadn't kept his new shoes on, and he'd said he would, but they'd been too special. She'd laughed at him and tickled him till he'd howled for mercy—and that was when they'd started *Oliver Twist*. She'd read to him after that. Sometimes. When her cough wasn't too bad. They hadn't actually finished it yet. Sam had never imagined himself as an orphan like Oliver. Other children were orphaned, not him.

He didn't feel much like reading it now after all. At least, not yet. He put it back and took out the other, his beloved *Travels of Mansa Musa* that he'd read at least three times already. He carried it over to the table, sat down, and smoothed out the first page.

"'My name is Mansa Musa,'" he read, his lips moving silently, though in truth he knew the familiar opening words of the book by heart now, he had read them so often. "'My name is Mansa Musa. I was born at a time when a man was a man and women were won by those who deserved them . . .'"

The sounds outside faded, the clatter of dishes, clucking of chickens, dogs barking, voices raised in laughter, all faded, and he was lost in the book with the great king, going on his travels, searching for his lost parents.

10

"THE LORD'S MY SHEPHERD, I'LL NOT WANT.

He makes me down to lie

In pastures green; He leadeth me,

The quiet waters by . . ."

Sam stopped so suddenly that Enock bumped into him. "Amai used to sing that," he told Ezelina beside him. And he'd hummed it with her sometimes.

She wasn't really listening to him. They were already hurrying to see what was going on. People were clustered at the open door to one of the wards, singing, and more singing was coming from inside the ward.

Sam squeezed through after the others until they were right inside. There were ten beds in the ward, all with children on them, some sitting, some lying down. Mats on which their mothers or guardians slept at night were rolled up on the floor. At each bed a guardian was opening a big plastic bag. They tipped out the contents, sending T-shirts and shorts and trousers, all sorts, tumbling out onto the beds. They picked them up and stroked them and held them up to the light to admire, all the time singing their praise.

It was a sign! It had to be. Probably all Sam had to do was go back to Aunt Mercy's, once they'd got the fish they'd been sent out for, and wait, and his shoes would come in a plastic bag like one of these, even if he wasn't sick or dying himself.

As the last verse died away, there was ululating from outside. Ezelina, Enock, and Sam wormed their way back, jumped off the verandah, and ran over. A group of older women in loose white blouses, with white doekies wrapped round their heads, were dancing, stamping the ground, bending, raising their arms again, twirling, singing, and making a high wailing noise. Ezelina was the first to join in as they launched into a song. She jumped into the middle of the circle, and then so did Enock and Sam, too, dancing with them. Sam got into the swing of it soon enough, stamping and bending, shaking and turning.

A van drew up. The rear doors opened, and more plastic bags were tossed out. The women stopped their dancing and caught them, then swung along to the next ward, Ezelina, Enock, and Sam with them.

Mr. Bwinji came out and stood at his door just as they were passing.

Sam smiled happily at him.

"Hello. Have you come back to help me?"

Sam grinned even more widely. "Sure." He was up on the verandah, in at the door, and seated at the keyboard in no time.

"Now, then. Show me how I change the size of the font. And you were going to put in page numbers for me."

It was good sitting there, showing Mr. Bwinji how to work the computer program. In the background the singing grew fainter as the women moved round the hospital.

"Can you show me how to get on to the Internet, too?" Mr. Bwinji asked, as Sam beavered away.

Sam saved the document and went into the desktop. "I don't think you can."

"Are you sure?"

"Yes." Sam nodded. He moved down the icons with the mouse, but the right icon wasn't there. "You need an Internet connection."

"Can you get one for me on the screen?"

"Uh-uh." Sam shook his head. "You have to have a telephone connection for that." He clicked on one of the icons, not really meaning to, and a list showed on the screen.

"A telephone connection," Mr. Bwinji repeated thoughtfully. "I haven't got access to one of those."

Sam looked up as someone leaned over him. It was the director. Sam hadn't heard him come in.

"Those files are confidential! Mr. Bwinji, I'm surprised at you. I thought we had discussed this. Off you go, my lad!"

Sam pushed back his chair, hurt. "I was only helping. I always helped Amai," he protested.

"Did you? Well, just at the moment we have other things to get on with. And this information"—he waved crossly at the screen—"is not for your eyes. Now scram!"

*   *   *

Organ music blared from the radio like the groans and sighs of the dead. Aunt Mercy had put the radio on the stool in front of her and turned it up as loud as it would go. She sat bolt upright on her stool in the doorway to the hut, listening. It was almost sunset, time for the day's death announcements. The organ chords trembled away, and a man's voice came on the air, calling out men's and women's names. With each name, Aunty clicked her tongue against her teeth.

Ezelina had taken over the cooking, and she was watching the pan of little gray fish that they were frying to have as relish with that evening's nsima.

Sam wandered over to the radio. "Did they read out Amai's name?"

Aunt Mercy turned down the volume a little. "What's that, my love?"

"Was my amai's name called out on the radio like that?" Sam repeated.

"Of course. How else did I know that she had passed over?"

"And that's when you went to town."

She nodded. "To bring you home here." She drew him to her and cuddled him.

He nestled against her side as the roll call of the dead rose and fell. He breathed in her smells, a mixture of the soap she'd just washed herself with and the stale sweat that clung still to her dress. Amai had smelled more of flowers, from the perfume that she sprayed on her wrists and behind her ears every morning. Sometimes he'd watched her. Sometimes she'd let him; other times she'd chased him away, threatening to spray him with the stuff till she'd collapsed into the nearest chair, laughing. Sometimes. Before she'd been unable to chase, before the day she'd gone to bed and stayed there, before she'd found it difficult to speak through the coughing, before she'd started to smell peculiar.

But Sam didn't want to remember that. He loosened himself from Aunt Mercy's embrace and moved right away from the radio, over to Enock and Macdonald, huddled over something under the tree, curious to see what it was.

"That's mine!" They looked up, surprised. "You've no right!" They had his *Travels of Mansa Musa*. "You never asked!" He tried to snatch the book. Behind him, the strains of the organ signaled that the day's announcements were over.

Macdonald held on tight, and there was a tussle till finally he gave way. "Take your stupid book! You wouldn't have given it to me if I had asked."

Sam clasped it safely to his chest "It's in English! I don't expect they teach English at the school here!" He was shouting at them.

Aunt Mercy was there beside them. "Macdonald, Enock—say you're sorry to Sammy for taking his book without asking."

They looked at each other in amazement.

"Now," she said, quietly and very firmly.

"I'm sorry," said Enock.

"Sorry," Macdonald muttered, staring at Sam.

Aunt Mercy nodded. "There, now. Sammy, come with me." She led the way into the hut.

"They shouldn't play with my book," he said crossly as he trailed after her. "That Macdonald took it from my case."

"Enough." She sighed heavily. "First it is your shoes, now it is this." She seemed to be thinking aloud. She plumped down on the edge of her bed and beckoned him till he was standing in front of her. "The book."

He was puzzled.

"Give me the book."

He handed it to her.

She put it on the bed beside her, rested her left hand on it. "Now, listen, young man. You do not know that Macdonald took it. For all you know, Enock did."

Sam opened his mouth to explain.

"Hush. I have not finished. You said Macdonald could not read English. He can. He is not doing at all badly at school. But he has no book of his own. Nor has Ezelina or Enock. Not a book like this. We have the family Bible, and that is all."

Sam knew about the Bible. It was kept on the shelf, wrapped carefully in a deep blue cloth. Every evening Aunt Mercy took it down and read from it.

"You must learn to share," she repeated. "You are not on your own here. You have been very fortunate, and now you must share some of that fortune with others."

He looked down, gave a little kick to the floor in frustration. His eyes were watering. *Fortunate?* With Amai dead and him here? And no running shoes?

"Look at me." Her voice was firm.

"But it's not fair!" he burst out. "It's my book!"

She gazed at him impassively till he dropped his eyes once more.

"I said you must learn to share. You live with other children here. Now. Please call in the others."

Sam shuffled to the door. "Hey, you! Ezelina, Enock, Macdonald! Aunty wants you!" and he turned back inside and waited.

When they were assembled, Aunt Mercy spoke. "From now on, Sam will share his book with you." She passed him the book.

He stared at her.

"It will live on the shelf," she went on. "Take turns reading it, and treat it carefully."

The others were quiet, listening.

"When you read it, I want you to do so inside, here at the table, and I want you always to wash your hands first. Is that clear?"

They nodded in turn. "Good. Macdonald, will you put the book on the shelf, please?"

Sam handed it over reluctantly to Macdonald, who took it, not looking at Sam, and went and put it on the shelf.

Aunt Mercy clapped her hands and levered herself off the bed. "Right. Now, out, all of you."

Macdonald, Enock, and Ezelina trooped after her. It was as dark outside now as inside, except for the glow of the cooking fire.

Quickly, Sam went to the shelf and moved his precious book from where Macdonald had placed it to beside his parents' photograph. If the book had to be shared by all of them equally, at least his parents would protect it for him if they could see it there. He looked round the room in case a plastic bag had magically appeared with his shoes in it. He even peered under the bed. There was no bag, not that he could see.

"*Muli bwanje?*" The older carpenter was in the shadows at the edge of their clearing as Sam came out.

"*Ndili bwino,*" they chorused, and "*Kaia inu.*"

Aunt Mercy walked her slow, stately walk across the yard to the man, skirting the cooking fire.

"*Ndili bwino, zikomo,*" he was answering.

"Come, come," said Aunt Mercy. "You must eat with us. Sam, fetch a stool."

"Did you know any of the names today?" asked the carpenter, nodding at the radio as he sat down. "Was there anyone who was close to you?"

"No one close, no. Two in the village have passed over. Remember Justice, the brother of . . ."

Sam let his mind drift away from the loud radio voice with the death announcements. At home he and Amai would have been drinking juice together at this hour. She would have told him the story of her day; there was always something funny to tell, like the time the tailor sewed the legs of some silk trousers shut. Or when the neighbor went into the lavatory and found a black mamba behind the door. . . .

". . . little Robbie at the doctors' has a fever."

Recognizing the name, Sam was brought out of his daydream.

"Ai-ee! That is bad," said the carpenter.

Aunt Mercy nodded. "I hope it is at worst malaria and nothing!" Her voice trailed away.

The carpenter *hmm-hmm*ed in agreement.

"They are doing tests." There was a silence. "We must pray that he will get better.

"Ezelina," Aunt Mercy called then. "Please bring water for our guest to wash his hands. Sam, you help her. Is the food ready, Ezelina?"

"Yes, Amai."

Ezelina fetched the plastic washing-up bowl and tossed a small clean towel at Sam. She ran water into the bowl from the tap and held it in front of the carpenter for him to wash his hands, and then Aunty. Sam followed Ezelina with the towel. But then he didn't know what to do with it. Enock took it from him, shaking his head pityingly, and hung it on a nail.

Once the meal was finished and they had prayed for little sick Robbie and the plates had been washed and put away, the carpenter cleared his throat. He looked at Sam.

"You are a lucky boy here with your aunt," he said. "She has done many good things!"

Sam nodded. He knew that. It's just that he wasn't much feeling it at the moment.

The man looked shrewdly at him. "Do you know the story of Kaumphawi?"

"Yes!" shouted Macdonald.

It must be a good story, then, thought Sam. "What is the story?" he asked.

Macdonald, Ezelina, and Enock came and sat nearer. Enock, who'd been looking after Chikondi, put him on his lap and crossed his arms round him. They were ready.

"You have your problems," the carpenter said to Sam. "We all have. I've heard about your shoes going. Even so . . ."

Macdonald was smiling a secret smile.

The carpenter cleared his throat and began: "Long ago there was a boy called Kaumphawi, the poor one. His father had died when he was little and his mother when he was still just a boy . . ."

Like me, thought Sam, sitting up straighter.

". . . brought up by his sister, who treated him like a slave, giving him just enough food so as not to starve. He was never allowed to wash at home but had to go to the stream even at the coldest time of year, as if he was a leper. He had to look after the cows and fetch water and gather wood, and he never had any time to play or to go to school."

Well, he'd gone gathering wood, too, thought Sam.

"One evening, unable to bear this any longer, Kaumphawi went to his mother's grave. He knelt beside it. 'Oh, Amai,' he said, 'I am so miserable,' and he told his mother all about his life since she was gone."

"*Ay-yai.* It is good that he could speak to his mother," said Macdonald. "It is good that he could go to her grave."

Sam hardly listened to the rest of the story, to how Amai's spirit changed into a python and came and punished Kaumphawi's wicked sister. The voices around him faded as he worried.

That was it. He wanted to be able to go and talk to Amai, to tell her about today, about helping the man with the computer. About being chased away, he thought glumly. About the stone. About sharing his book, and about his running shoes. Aunt Mercy hadn't said she'd buy him another pair. Even if she had, where would they buy them? There weren't any shoe shops around the village. Maybe he could ask her to write to Mr. Gunya for him to send some.

Amai would have told him what to do. If only he could talk to her.

But how could he? Her grave wasn't here. Her body was under the earth in town, many miles away—another way of life, another world away, far from their ancestors. How would her spirit ever find him here? If he spoke to her, how would she hear him?

Lying on his mat that night in the deep darkness, the window and door shut and bolted, and the only sound from outside was the yipping and yapping of dogs, Sam remembered his parents' photograph. Of course! They would be watching over him from the top of the cupboard, through the darkness, just as they were protecting his book. He turned on his side, smiling.

Then he went cold inside. Could they really see him? Could they? After all, that photograph was taken when they married, which was two years before he was born. They hadn't even been thinking about him then, so how could the spirits in the photograph know him and watch over him? If only his mother had been buried here where she belonged, he could have gone and talked to her. If his mother had been buried here, she could turn into a python, too, and go sliding over the ground to whoever had taken his shoes and crush them.

How could she not have chosen to be buried here with her ancestors? How?

11

SAM SWUNG THE BANANAS FROM THEIR STUMPY STALK.
He'd offered to fetch them and had gone on his own this time,
wanting to show that he knew what to do.

But there was no one outside the hut when he returned,
which was odd. When he'd left, walking as far as the market
with Aunt Mercy, not even very long ago, Macdonald and
Ezelina and Enock and Chikondi had all been there.

He heard giggling, and it seemed to be coming from
inside. At the door he stopped. There was a gaggle of children, some he thought he recognized, some he didn't, and
some had their backs to him anyway. He wanted to see what
they were laughing at.

In the middle of the group, Macdonald was strutting
about, clowning. Ezelina was giggling, a hand over her
mouth.

Sensing that someone new was there, Macdonald turned
and peered into the doorway where Sam was silhouetted
against the sunshine. "Go away," he mouthed when he saw it
was Sam.

Ezelina caught sight of Sam, too. "He doesn't have to go."

"Yes, he does. He isn't one of us. Anyway, all he cares
about are those shoes of his."

No one else looked round, none of them bothered. "Go on, Macdonald!" they called. "Don't stop!"

Sam dumped the bananas on the windowsill, backed off, and wandered along the track he was getting to know best. Outside the bungalow he stopped. He first looked warily at the stone and nodded to it respectfully. Then he gazed up at the bungalow. He would have quite liked to go in, to see if it looked like home there, too. Maybe if he asked Aunt Mercy, she would let him, even though she didn't let the twins—and maybe she would shut up the dog first After all, it was the sort of house he knew.

A man appeared with garden shears. *Snap,* they went on branches in the hedge. *Snap, snap.*

Sam glanced at him, then back at the bungalow. *That room at the front could be a bedroom,* he thought. The curtains at the window were even a pinky-red, almost like Amai's. A woman walked past the window on the other side, Robbie in her arms. A pale woman with dark hair tied back off her face.

"What are you looking at?"

"*Muli bwanje,*" Sam answered automatically, registering annoyance in the man's tone.

The gardener didn't respond. "Don't hang about here," he said. "Go and hang about somewhere else. This is the doctors' house, you've no business here. Go on!" He waved the shears threateningly in the air.

Sam trailed off unhappily. The man had treated him like

any lowlife. Couldn't he tell that Sam belonged in a house like that?

The stone nearly tripped him up again. "Please let me pass," he muttered, not stopping. His feet led him to the one place where he might be welcome.

But when he got to Mr. Bwinji's office at the hospital, the door to the verandah stood open, and the room was empty. The laptop was on the desk, open, and it was on.

Sam entered. He went to the inner door and listened. No one was coming. He pulled up a chair. He ran his fingertips gently over the keys, enjoying the familiar feel of them. If only he'd brought Invaders 3 with him! He could have slotted it in and played it.

Footsteps.

Firm footsteps, hard soles, coming closer down the passage.

Sam shot out of the chair and back out onto the verandah. He didn't stop till he reached the gateway of the hospital that arched over the drive.

Nonchalantly, he bent and scratched his foot, though it wasn't itching.

"Hey, Sam!"

He looked up, surprised. Enock was waving at him. He was holding a small paper bag.

"What've you got? Let's have a look."

"Eggs. Careful!"

Sam got into step beside Enock, pleased to be with him.

"Come!" Enock beckoned, darting over to a hut they were passing. He stepped onto a big stone just to the left of the window opening and pointed to the space beside him.

"Look," he said, as Sam squeezed up on the stone.

At first Sam couldn't see because it was dark in the hut. As his eyes adjusted, he made out a sleeping mat with a bundle on it. The bundle took on the form of a man. The man's face showed above the flimsy cover. It was cracked and emaciated.

They stood there in silence, looking. Sam tried not to breathe in. The smell from the dying man was fetid and foul, worse than his mother's had been. A nurse had come in every day to wash Amai. He didn't know if anyone had come to wash this man.

They dropped back to the ground at the same time. "You breathed it in!" Enock said. "I heard you. Maybe you'll get the Disease now!"

"Maybe I won't." Sam faced him fair and square on the path. "That's not how you get it."

"How, then?" Enock challenged.

"Men and women get it when they have sex."

"All right, town boy, just checking!" and Enock ran, eggs clutched to his chest for safety.

Sam ran after him. "Do you know why your atate died?"

"Oh, like everyone. He got weaker and weaker, and then he was bewitched and he died."

"Why was he bewitched?"

"I dunno. Amai says she expects it's because he went to town."

Sam digested this. "My amai didn't die because she was bewitched, and she lived in town," he said. "She died because she got the Disease."

"So how did she get the Disease?" Enock challenged him.

"From sex. I told you," he muttered. "From Atate." A lump sprang into his throat. He swallowed hard to fight it down. "Do you go and talk to your father?"

Enock shrugged. "Sometimes. Not as often as I used to," he added. "But his spirit doesn't have far to travel. He knows where I am."

Sam blinked hard. "Where is he? I mean, where is his grave?"

"Shall I show you?"

Sam nodded.

Enock led him down a track to the left. Trees grew so tall on either side that only speckles of sunlight were able to pattern the dirt road here. There were no houses or huts. The dying man's had been the last one. Finally, they reached the graveyard, up a gentle slope. It was shaded and dark under the high trees. No sunlight at all came through to shine on the white stones that marked the edges of the graves, no light illumined the names on the headstones, so Sam had to peer at the names and the recent dates. Here and there as they passed, no grass and plants had yet grown round a grave, and the earth over these looked fresher.

Enock threaded his way through the graves to the top of the slope, up in the far corner. "Here," he said, stopping. "Here's Atate." He bowed his head, and his lips moved silently. Then, "This is Sam," he said out loud. "He's come to live with us."

Sam wasn't sure quite what to do. He glanced at Enock, but Enock didn't help. *Muli bwanje,* Sam said.

Silence.

Enock nudged him and led the way back to the track. He set off half-skipping, holding the bag of eggs close to his chest as if he hadn't a care in the world. He turned when he realized Sam wasn't following. "Aren't you coming?" he called.

Sam shook his head. All the graves, all the dead people in them, Atate, Amai, not here but under graves, too, buried under earth and heavy stone. He kept his face averted. "I'll stay a bit."

"You can't."

"Why not?"

"The spirits will come for you." Enock looked round.

Sam looked round, too. The trees were close and dark, but here, on the edge, surely he'd be safe.

Enock looked as if he was about to object again. Instead, he gave Sam a lopsided grin and, as he stepped on the track to take back the eggs, said "Just be careful" over his shoulder.

And then the tears came. Sam didn't try to stop them now. He didn't remember his atate all that well, it was Amai in his mind all the time, it was Amai he needed. Why wasn't he able to talk to her? Enock could talk to his atate; why couldn't Sam talk to Amai?

Slowly, his sobbing eased. His chest no longer felt quite so tight. He sat there, feeling empty, on a stone where the graveyard met the track with his back to the graves. His spine prickled. Maybe a spirit was behind him, Enock's father's spirit. His heart raced. He glanced to the side, but there was nothing, nothing hovered above the stone slabs.

Sam snapped his head round. No spirit was there, either, creeping up behind him. "Whew." He breathed out, relieved. He raised his face to the sky, but the trees were in the way.

The trees! They were moving, their branches were reaching down to him, slowly, languorously, brown wood fingers, green fingertips waving in the breeze, bending at the waists of their trunks, coming nearer.

Not possible.

He squeezed his eyes shut, looked again.

There was nothing. Just the rustling of leaves.

It was so dark here. Sam stood up to go, looking bravely at the trees. He fancied that they moved again. They were coming for him, he shouldn't be there, his amai's spirit wasn't there.

He fled, not really knowing where he was going, hoping he'd catch up with Enock. But the dying man's hut didn't appear. He found he was wading through flat tea bushes that reached up to his waist. Twigs scratched him. *Like the bones of dead men's fingers,* he thought. No. He shook himself. Surely there was no shelter for spirits here, good ones or bad, and the bushes stretched for miles.

He began to feel safer. It was easy to walk between the bushes, even where there wasn't a path. Strange to think that these dark green leaves could end up as tea. Aunt Mercy said there was a tea factory near the boma, where the local government offices were. It wasn't far away but she'd never been there, which probably meant that he would never go, either.

He kicked a nearby bush, then looked round guiltily. He felt suddenly frightened again; what if he was wrong, and there *was* a spirit watching? He heard a thrumming noise, and his heart started to thud wildly. A motorbike was advancing fast among the bushes. He kept his head down, in case the rider had seen him hitting the bush, and walked on steadily, biting the inside of his cheek.

The motorbike stopped.

"Can't you hear? You deaf or something?"

The man had stopped and was beckoning him. He pushed up the bottom part of his helmet. "Am I going the right way to the mission?" he asked as Sam wound his way through bushes toward the track where he waited.

Sam nodded, but he wasn't looking at the man. His eyes were riveted on the motorbike. It was huge and black. Even through the powdering of red dust Sam could see that it looked brand-new.

The man took off his helmet. He rubbed his head hard, wiped sweat off his forehead. His face was long, and his skin was a bit lighter than most people's, like the woman who advertised Sparkie, Sam thought. Maybe from wearing a helmet and being protected like that from the sun. And he had sticking-out ears.

"Well? What are you doing out here? If you live at the mission, I can give you a lift home." The man's eyes were calm and shrewd.

Sam felt a jolt. In a flash, his fear was forgotten. This was no spirit. A lift on the bike? It had a seat behind. "It's a BMW," he said in awe. As Atate's car had been before his mother had sold it for the Ford.

"Know something about motorbikes, do you?"

Sam nodded. In fact, he'd just read the letters at the side part of the front, inside the round badge, but he wasn't going to say so.

"If you live at the mission," the man went on, "what were you doing going in the other direction?" He looked more closely at Sam. "Ah. What's your name?"

"Samuel Sangala."

"Well, I'm Allan. Allan Poot." He put out a hand.

"*Muli bwanje,*" said Sam, quickly remembering his manners and shaking the hand that was offered.

They exchanged greetings.

"Come on, Samuel. I'll take you back to your mother."

Sam frowned. "Amai's late. And people call me Sam."

"Ah. Then who is it that you're living with, Sam?"

"Aunt Mercy."

"So hop on behind, and show me where your aunt Mercy lives."

"Don't you know?" Surely everyone at the mission knew that.

"I'm not from round here," said Allan. "When I was about your age, my parents took me to Holland."

Sam looked up. Why Holland? Perhaps it was rude to ask, he thought, so he didn't.

Allan told him anyway. "That's where they'd met when my father went there to study. Then when they came back here, she missed Holland. It was her country, they were her people," he said, half to himself. "But in Holland my father missed Malawi, so in the end we came back home."

"Did your mother come, too?"

He shook his head. "She died."

Allan shook himself, as if to shake off a difficult memory, like a dog when it comes out of water, or so it seemed to Sam. "Because I'd been a boy in another country," Allan went on, "I was curious when we came back here. So I'm traveling round, working in different places, each place for a year or so.

"But that's enough about me. Come on, young man, let's take you home. Hop on. You'll have to show me the way."

Sam scrambled up behind on the wide pillion and put his hands on the man's waist. He watched as Allan swiftly turned a key, pushed a button, then twisted the right handle and pulled in the left, pressed his left foot down on a pedal, and they were away.

"Hold on tight!" Allan called over his shoulder. "It's bumpy. We don't want you falling off."

With the thrum of the machine beneath him and the air rushing past, Sam felt as if he was flying. This was the way to travel! One day, he vowed, he'd have a motorbike, too.

They drove into a small cloud of midges, and he brushed them off his cheeks. "Don't let go!" shouted the man.

"This way!" Sam called above the roar of the engine as they reached the first houses of the mission settlement. They swerved to avoid a bicycle ambulance that suddenly appeared from a path at the side, a man steadily pedaling the patient on it. Sam spluttered and spat, this time not moving his hands. When he'd opened his mouth, a fly had flown straight into it.

Allan slowed down and puttered through the outside waiting room, scattering the chickens.

A small brown mongrel, wandering along the hospital verandah, jumped down and raced toward them, yapping. It ran on alongside, trying to nip Sam's ankles but failing because every time it got too close Sam kicked out at it and it had to keep dodging his kicking feet. Beyond the dog, Sam could see the patients and their guardians gazing at them, and his chest swelled with pride. Two boys ran alongside, whooping, and were soon joined by others. Sam took one hand off and waved wildly until he decided it would be more dignified to look straight ahead and act as if he rode pillion every day of his life. He felt like a chief up there on the shiny black steed. "Left here!" Sam called as they reached the last ward of the hospital.

The dog kept pace with them, barking, all the way to the market, where it saw them off to its satisfaction, loosing a volley of barks at them when Allan turned off right to Aunt Mercy's, as Sam instructed.

"Here!" he called over the engine noise. "Stop!"

Allan gave him a thumbs-up to show he'd heard, revved the engine a bit harder, and skidded to a dramatic stop in a swirl of red dust at the edge of Aunt Mercy's place.

Ezelina was there, washing clothes by the tap in their two plastic bowls, and Chikondi and Enock were there, too, back with the eggs. They stared at him, their eyes as round as plums. Enock ran over as Sam put one foot to the ground and slid off the pillion.

"Oh, what a big machine. It must be good to ride on." Enock stroked the leather seat reverently.

Allan raised his visor, smiling. "*Muli bwanje*, young man."

Enock repeated the greeting in a rush. Then, again, "It is good to ride on, is it not?"

Allan nodded, but he didn't offer a ride.

Enock's face fell. Sam grinned. He'd been the lucky one.

"I have tea to deliver to the hospital," Allan said, "but"—

and he pulled his visor back down—"I tell you what"—as he turned the motorbike—"I'll come back sometime and take you for a ride. And you again, young Sam."

"And me?" shouted Ezelina.

Macdonald turned up soon afterwards. Enock rushed out at him. "Sam came home on the back of a motorbike. It was huge, really black and shiny!"

"So I heard. People told me."

Enock didn't seem to hear the sour note in Macdonald's voice. He went on excitedly, "And the man's—what's his name, Sam?"

"Allan Poot," said Sam.

"That's right, the man, Allan, he says he'll come back and give us all rides."

"Not me, though. I wasn't here," Macdonald said grumpily.

"Well, I'm sure he means you, too. Doesn't he, Sam?"

Sam pretended not to hear.

When he unrolled his mat and lay down to sleep that night, it was the motorbike that he saw and felt, the wind on his cheeks and the thrumming of the engine as it hurtled him toward sleep.

12

THE NEXT DAY ALL OF THEM SET OUT TO GATHER FIRE-
wood. The sun bounced off the red earth of the road, loosening its rich, musty smell, and the splodges of brighter red
from the geraniums, carefully tended outside the brick and
mud huts, were cheerful and fresh.

Even Macdonald wasn't being grumpy with Sam this
morning. He'd greeted him and was now including him in
the conversation as they walked. "And in South Africa you
can live in a big city with buildings as high as—as high
as . . ." He was struggling to find a comparison.

"As high as . . . that tree," suggested Enock, pointing at
the tree above their heads with the sun sending darts of light
through the top leaves.

"Higher," said Ezelina, head thrown back, eyes narrowed.

"Much higher," said Sam. "As high as . . ." But he
couldn't find a comparison either.

"As Mount Mandingwe!" Enock cried.

They stopped and looked doubtfully at the mountain, its
top veiled in wispy cloud.

Sam knew that the buildings in South Africa were very
tall—in Johannesburg, at any rate; he'd seen pictures of

them in his father's books at home. There'd been no buildings like them in Blantyre.

"That's where I want to go," boasted Macdonald. "Mavuto's going to get work."

"That Mavuto!" Enock laughed.

"He's full of talk." Ezelina frowned. "How's he going to get a job there?"

"I don't know. He says so. Maybe I'll go with him."

"Have you told my amai?" Enock challenged him.

Macdonald shook his head. "No. Anyway, I haven't gone yet, have I?"

"Let's get the sticks from the field beyond the graveyard," said Enock.

"Which graveyard?" Macdonald stopped. "The one where your atate is? I'm not going there."

But the "there" came out funny because with a squeal and a clatter a bicycle was on them. It was Mavuto. As he took his feet off the pedals and dragged them along the ground to brake, his wheel had nudged the back of Macdonald's leg.

"Hello, Mavuto."

Macdonald, grinning, slapped Mavuto on the shoulder.

"Hello." Mavuto greeted them all abruptly, slapping Macdonald in turn.

"Macdonald says you're going to work in South Africa," Enock said.

Mavuto thought for a moment. "Sure. Maybe," he boasted. "Well, one day. You coming, Macdonald?"

Macdonald barely hesitated before jumping onto the luggage carrier behind him. "Where to?"

"Around," said Mavuto, waving an arm vaguely in the air, wheeling, and starting to cycle back down the track.

Ezelina stared after them, hands on hips. Chikondi was clapping his hands. "Do you want to go with them, too?" she asked him, reaching back and gently tugging one of his ears. He gurgled at her.

"Oh, come on, Ezza," Enock said. "We don't need them."

"I didn't say we did. But when did Macdonald last fetch firewood?"

"Dunno."

"Well, it's not fair. Amai says his father was really lazy, too."

"Is his father our uncle?" Sam asked.

"No, he's not really family. Amai says that he's the son of . . . Whose son is he, Ezza?" asked Enock.

Ezza didn't answer. They were going past the graveyard now. Her lips moved silently; Enock's, too. Sam looked fearfully up at the trees, then quickly lowered his head in respect.

"The son of Sam's mother's cousin." Ezelina continued the earlier conversation.

"But he isn't really," said Enock.

"Oh, Enock, does it matter? He's the son of a neighbor of hers who's sick."

"She isn't sick, Ezza."

"She is."

Sam was surprised. He hadn't heard the twins argue before.

"But not just!"

"Enock," Ezelina said warningly.

"She's a witch. She poisoned her brother-in-law."

"Poisoned!" exclaimed Sam.

"Well, that's what they say," Ezelina admitted grudgingly. "But Amai says she isn't a witch. She says it's just jealousy."

"Who?" Sam was confused.

"The brother-in-law's sister," said Enock. "And she burned Macdonald's cheek."

"Amai says that was an accident."

"And his wife put a curse on her," Enock went on, ignoring Ezelina's interruption. "Anyway," he finished, "she's sick now. And Macdonald is with us."

"How long for?" Sam wanted to know.

"Maybe always, I don't know."

"So Macdonald isn't really your cousin at all." Sam wanted to get this straight. It would make a difference, he thought, make Macdonald less important.

Enock shook his head. "But it doesn't matter. We call him family."

Sam changed the subject. "How far are we going? Can't we stop here?"

"We-ell . . ." Enock didn't seem to want to. He and Ezelina exchanged quick glances.

"I suppose it's all right," Ezelina said firmly in the end, loosening her cloth and lowering Chikondi to the ground.

The three of them searched and gathered wood in silence, first taking the sticks back to Chikondi and setting them in a neat pile. But Chikondi messed up the pile, taking out one stick after another to play with. Ezelina gave up trying to stop him.

Sam moved on, picking up sticks, leaving them in small bundles as he went, and going forward. To his side, Enock was doing the same. Ezelina was over to the left now with Chikondi, who'd toddled after her. Another stick, and another, and another.

Sam came up against a tangle of trees, branches wildly interlocked, leaves growing thickly. It made a dense hedge, too dark and deep to look through. He straightened to look over it and see what was on the other side, expecting it to be the graveyard where the twins' father was buried. But that was over behind him. The hedge was higher than he was, taller even than Macdonald if Macdonald had been with them, as tall as trees. It stretched sideways, to his left and to his right, like a ragged, thick green wall.

He dropped the sticks he was holding and crept along the hedge to the right. He wanted to see what was on the other side.

"Sam!" Enock called. It was a funny call, like a very loud whisper.

Still examining the hedge, he only half-turned. "Yes?"

"Let's take back the sticks."

"In a moment." Sam continued along, looking for a gap in the growth.

"No, now!"

Sam turned when he heard the almost panicky note in Enock's voice. "Why?"

"Just because."

"Why?"

"We're not supposed to be here."

"But you brought me here for wood."

"No—*here,* I mean. Here at the edge."

"Why not?"

"This is as far as we should go. No farther."

"Why not? You brought me to your atate's graveyard."

"This isn't the graveyard."

"It's near."

"But it isn't the same. The carpenter says that if we go farther here, we'll—we'll be hexed, we'll go mad." Enock winced at the thought.

"Who's 'we'?"

"We from the village, of course. He says we're too young." Enock turned and beckoned Sam to follow. "Come on. Let's get back to Ezza."

Sam went along with Enock. This time, he thought, Enock was serious. This time it wasn't a tease, he wasn't testing Sam or anything.

He turned slowly. As he bent to pick up the first group of sticks he'd left on the ground, he looked back over his shoulder. The hedge looked safer from here. They'd had a hedge at home, at the back of their garden. All right, it wasn't as high as this one, and it had been neatly trimmed like the doctors', but it was a hedge just the same.

What harm could a hedge do?

13

SAM HELPED THE TWINS PILE THE FIREWOOD NEATLY beside the door. They wouldn't need to go for more for a few days.

At home Sam would have played computer games now. Or gone out to see a friend.

He stood there, irresolute. Sat down, stood up again, and went to fetch his Game Boy. He sat on the ground, leaning against the mango tree, turned it on, and began pressing keys. He became absorbed in his game, and even when Enock came over and stood at his shoulder, watching, he didn't stop. He didn't think Enock would know how to play, but he wasn't going to offer to show him, at least not right at this moment.

Just as Sam reached a good score of 10,000, Macdonald appeared. A small torn sack was flung over his shoulder. Smiling oddly, he went into the house and came back without it, heading toward them. Sam decided to take his Game Boy in; he didn't want Macdonald playing it. He turned it off and went indoors and tossed it in his case. As he was closing the case, he caught sight of the sack, stuffed in the corner. He went over and prodded.

There were two things inside.

He hesitated, listening. He couldn't hear anyone coming,

only the sound of voices. Quickly, he untied the loose string at the sack's neck and put in his hand. A shoe came out, a bit grubby but still a bright blue. And a second, with a grass stain on the toe.

A wave of anger tore up at Sam from his belly. He grabbed the shoes, one in each hand, and went to the door, brandishing them. Outside, Macdonald was sitting a little apart from the others, not doing anything, apparently brooding.

Sam rushed at him. He was hitting Macdonald with the shoes before Macdonald had even seen him coming. "Thief! You thieved them! Thief!"

Macdonald put his hands up, trying to keep the shoes from hitting him. He caught one, scrambled to his feet, and swiped it at Sam's arm.

"Stop! I'll explain."

"Explain what? Thief! Thief!" Sam jabbed at Macdonald with the one shoe, *jab, jab.*

Macdonald held him off with one arm. They stood rigid, snarling at each other like dogs, as the others watched open-mouthed in amazement. Then Sam broke free and jabbed at a soft place. Macdonald let out a roar. With one twist, he had Sam on the ground and was on top of him. He dropped the shoe and pinned Sam's arms to the ground.

Sam kicked and bucked but couldn't get at Macdonald. He tried to butt him with his head, but Macdonald was too quick. He drew back his hand and slapped Sam's cheek. "Spoiled townie." He glared at him for a long moment. Then he spat on the ground beside Sam's ear, climbed off him, and stalked away.

Sam lay still. He rubbed his cheek, burning from the slap. Then Ezza was there, helping him to his feet. Enock ran off after Macdonald, calling out to him as he went.

"What was all that about?" asked Ezelina.

"He's a thief!"

"Macdonald?" She looked puzzled. "I don't think so."

"He took my shoes."

"Of course he didn't," Ezelina said. "Macdonald wouldn't do that."

But Sam had seen a shadow flit across her face, as if for a moment she wasn't entirely sure.

"He's not a thief," she repeated stoutly.

"Who is not a thief?" It was Aunty. None of them had noticed her arrival. "What is going on here?" She dropped her bag on the ground. "I have enough trouble with little Robbie without you adding to it. Sammy, why is the yard not swept? Ezelina, why is the fire not laid? Where is Enock? Hush now." She picked up Chikondi and cuddled him to stop his crying. "Well?" she asked, when no one answered.

"Enock went after Macdonald." Ezelina looked down at the ground.

Only Sam met Aunt Mercy's eyes. "Macdonald thieved my running shoes," he said.

"Did Macdonald say so?" Her voice sounded as hard as a stick of bamboo.

Under her steady gaze, Sam dropped his eyes. He shook his head.

"Until Macdonald comes back and we can talk to him about this, you will go inside and wait," she said to Sam.

"That's not fair—" Sam began to protest.

"Now," she said, pointing to the door, her arm rigid.

Sam took the sack that Ezelina held out to him.

He felt lonelier than ever. In the house he reached into the sack for the shoes, put them in his case, and turned the key in the lock. He stayed there, sitting on the concrete floor beside it, tears welling from his eyes. One dripped out, and another. He wiped them away with the back of his hand. He hated Macdonald. Macdonald had never liked him. Sam remembered Macdonald's half-smile, half-sneer when he'd turned up with the sack. It was so unfair. Sam had done nothing wrong, but Aunt Mercy was punishing him. He hadn't even made any more fuss about the shoes. "I've done nothing." He looked up at his parents' photograph and whispered it aloud.

But his father just stared out of the frame, and his mother, too, more shyly. "It's not fair!" he hissed at them. Still they just stared impassively. "Oh!" He whirled, sat on Aunt Mercy's bed, beat its edge with his fists in an agony of frustration. Tears fell again. He didn't know what bothered him more, the unfairness of it all, or Aunt Mercy's crossness and his being sent indoors, or his parents in the photograph not reacting.

He replayed the scene in his mind. Macdonald was a liar.

Sam had thought so from the start. Of course he was. Suddenly, Sam knew what he had to do: go and find Macdonald. He couldn't just wait here for him to come back.

He got up and peeped through the window. There was no one looking. Holding his breath, he slipped out. No one noticed. Enock had come back and was breaking sticks for the fire, Ezza and Aunt Mercy were sitting quietly talking. There was no sign of Macdonald.

One stride, two, and Sam was round the side of the house. No one saw him. He skirted the outside latrine and the small plot of tall leafy corn, Aunt Mercy's pride and joy, and was round the next house and onto the track. He walked fast away from the others, toward the market, the school, the church, past the first lot of hospital buildings. He knew the way now, needed no one to show him. He kept his eyes on his feet, bare this time, not wanting to catch anyone's eye, thinking hard.

Someone was walking beside him. Black leather shoes.

Sam looked up. Black trousers and shirt, a white dog collar. It was the minister from the church.

"Muli bwanje," Sam said quickly.

"Good afternoon. Are you well?"

"I am well if you are well."

"I am well, *zikomo,* thank you." And then, "You must be Mercy's Sammy."

Sam nearly corrected him but didn't quite dare. He felt shy with the minister. The last minister he'd been near had been praying over Amai in her grave.

"Let me walk a little way with you. Are you settling down well at Mercy Mlanga's? Getting on well with the others, are you, hmm?"

Sam nodded vaguely.

"Good, good. And where are you off to now?"

Sam shrugged.

"That is no answer." The minister's voice was a little sharp.

"I'm going after Macdonald," Sam answered a little sullenly.

"Ah, Macdonald. I know his family well. Such a tragedy, such a tragedy."

Sam didn't care about Macdonald's tragedy.

"I expect that you are fetching him home for supper."

Sam looked sideways and sort of nodded. He felt uneasy. He wasn't sure about fibbing to a minister. Perhaps, though, because he hadn't actually opened his mouth and said "yes," it was all right. "I have to go now."

"Fine, fine," said the minister. "I look forward to seeing you in church. Goodbye, until then. Be good. Goodbye, goodbye."

"Goodbye," Sam said back quickly, before the minister could say it again, and he set off at a trot to put distance between him and his fib.

Brown was the person he wanted to see. Brown wasn't family. They didn't really know each other, but Sam thought Brown liked him.

When he reached the green slope, there were the patients with their guardians in clusters on the grass. Someone had already lit a big cooking fire. Sam searched among them. One man was up nearer the laundry area, seated on a cloth, a woman beside him who looked like the guardian Sam had seen earlier. From the back, though, the man looked even older than Brown. He was all huddled up.

Sam left the track and went up the grass toward the old man, circling round so that he could see his face. It was indeed Brown. At the moment that Sam faced him, the old man noticed him, too. He straightened his back and smiled, and the smile made him look less ill, more like the man Sam had met with Ezelina.

"Come, come." Brown beckoned.

Sam went over and they exchanged greetings.

Stella got up. "You stay here for a moment with my father. You can keep him company while I help prepare the food."

"It was you yesterday on the motorbike," the old man said. "I heard all about it, big boy." He chuckled.

Sam grinned. But that had been yesterday. Now it was today, and things were different. His smile faded. Besides, he was getting alarmed; Brown's chuckles had turned to a hollow coughing that racked his whole body.

At last the coughing stopped. Brown closed his eyes, the better to gather up his strength once more. Then he opened them and peered shrewdly at Sam through milky eyes. "Is there something that you want to tell me? Is that why you have come?"

Sam hesitated, then nodded. "If someone stole your favorite things and you found out who it was, what would you do?"

"What does your aunty say?"

Sam squirmed. He didn't answer.

Brown was silent for some time. At last he opened his mouth. "Perhaps that would depend on how much I needed them in the first place."

"Would you ask the nchimi for a spell?"

Brown frowned.

Out of the corner of his eye, Sam saw a familiar shape lope past. "Macdonald!" he shouted. "Would you ask the nchimi for a spell?" he asked again, keeping an eye on where Macdonald was going.

Brown was still frowning. "What was it that was stolen?" But he was speaking to the air, because Sam was running, dodging the groups on the ground, running, the brown mongrel yapping at his heels, running to catch up with Macdonald.

At the corner Macdonald stopped so suddenly that Sam banged into him.

"Why did you steal them, thief? Why?"

"I told you, I'm no thief," Macdonald said, fiercely this time.

"I don't believe you."

"Don't, then. I don't care. Look at you. You come here with your expensive shoes. So cool, so different. You think you're better than everyone here. You understand nothing! Till you came we were happy. Why don't you go home!"

"Go home yourself," Sam retorted.

"I can't. Anyway, I was here before you." Macdonald turned away and set off back toward Aunt Mercy's before Sam could stop him.

Sam stamped his foot in frustration but let Macdonald go. Sam went off in the opposite direction, tears pricking the backs of his eyelids. Turned left. A calabash lay on the track at the side of the graveyard to collect coins to help with funeral costs. Sam stopped and began counting the kwachas that passersby had dropped into it. For one long awful moment he considered taking the coins.

If he did, he might be cursed. He left them alone.

Sam glanced left into the graveyard. Maybe he'd go and talk to Enock and Ezza's father, his uncle-by-marriage.

He stepped toward the nearest grave and realized that he didn't dare go any farther. He'd never get as far as where Enock had taken him, not now that he was on his own. He looked down at the grave next to his foot. June, the previous year. The person in it had died in June. The same month that Amai had passed over. He read the name on the stone: SALVATION MALIRO.

"*Muli bwanje*, Salvation Maliro." He went through the

rest of the greeting in his mind, his lips moving. *Ndili bwino, zikomo*. I'm well, thank you.

But Salvation wasn't well. How could he be, when he was dead?

"If you see my amai," Sam went on swiftly anyway, "please tell her I want to go home. I don't like it here. They take my shoes, they take my book, I sleep on the ground . . ."

He would have continued, but just at that moment someone passed slowly on the track just behind him. He scratched his head, pretending that he hadn't been talking. For all he knew, Salvation Maliro could be family of the person behind him, someone who might even mind him talking there.

112 When he got back to Aunt Mercy's, Sam managed to skirt the hut. He went into the latrine and came straight out again, letting the thin wooden door rattle loudly behind him.

He rounded the hut. The door was open. Inside, Aunt Mercy was talking to Macdonald.

Aunty broke off. "Come here, Sammy. Where were you? I thought I told you to stay inside."

"I had to go to the lav."

"Did you now?" Aunty waited for more of an explanation.

Sam didn't give one. He held his breath, expecting Macdonald to tell on him.

But Macdonald didn't.

Aunt Mercy switched her attention to Macdonald.

"Now, Macdonald. Sammy thinks that you stole his shoes. Did you?"

Why bother asking him, Sam wondered. He'd only say he didn't. Again.

"No." Macdonald kept his eyes on the ground.

There now! Sam felt almost triumphant at being proved right.

"Very well," said Aunt Mercy after a small silence. "Now, Sammy. Macdonald has said no. And you have your shoes back. Perhaps it is time to bury this issue. Say you are sorry."

Inside, Sam boiled. Everyone seemed to be on Macdonald's side, no one on his. He wouldn't say sorry. He didn't feel he'd done wrong.

Macdonald didn't apologize, either.

After a long wait Aunt Mercy simply got to her feet and walked out, leaving the two of them there.

Somehow that was worse than if she'd insisted on the apologies.

Macdonald fidgeted, then followed her.

Sam felt all at sea, cut adrift, unsure what to do. He thought he might cry.

He glanced up at the shelf. His eyes slid over the photograph to the book beside it.

Swallowing hard, he fetched *The Travels of Mansa Musa* and took it to the table to read, and soon he lost himself in the familiar story. Kankan, the boy who was to become Mansa, was being told off by the nomad Tariq, who'd rescued him from slavery: "I bought your freedom with gold. . . . I offered you a camel, but you chose to walk like a slave. . . . You claim to be a man but have not yet mastered the beast within you." Dignity was necessary, Tariq told him.

Dignity? Atate had had dignity. Amai had always said so, with pride in her voice. Maybe Atate had learned that in the desert. In any case, he'd never heard of Atate fighting. Maybe that was what dignity was about, not fighting.

The smell of cooking curled inside the hut. Sam's nose twitched. He heard voices rising, a man's voice among them. He closed the book and put it back.

When he emerged, the carpenter was there and was telling a story. "The chameleon escaped by climbing to the top of the tree. He called to God to follow him, but God . . ."

They were all gathered round the fire—Macdonald, too. Aunt Mercy motioned Sam forward to join the group. He squatted, eyes lowered, and took the plate she passed him. The others' eyes swiveled to Sam, then back to the carpenter as he went on with the story.

". . . but God answered that he was too old to climb. When the spider heard this, he spun a fine thread and lifted God to safety. . . ." Smoke from the fire changed direction and floated into Sam's face, stinging his eyes. He wiped them and looked away.

At the edge of the light cast by the fire, leaning on the saddle of his bicycle, stood Mavuto, with longing in his eyes.

14

"ARE WE GOING TO SCHOOL?" SAM ASKED.

Ezelina was pulling on a navy blue skirt over a smart white blouse.

"No, silly, it's the holidays, isn't it?"

Enock laughed at Sam. But he, too, was putting on school uniform. "It's Sunday."

"Oh." For a moment Sam was disappointed. He'd have quite liked to have gone to school. He was pretty sure he'd be top of the class. St. Mungo's in town was bound to be better than any village school.

"Get dressed, Sam. Come on—hurry up." Aunt Mercy had on her long skirt with a flounce round the bottom and was tying a white doekie round her hair. "Put on a clean pair of shorts and a shirt," she said. "They're still in your case."

Church, Sam thought. *Of course.*

"After you have washed! And in church I should like you all to pray for the safe recovery of Robbie."

"Will he be all right?" Ezelina asked.

"It is malaria. We pray that he will be. They are giving him the right pills."

They walked to church in a group, joining other families and groups, up the path lined with whitewashed stones and into the large, cool interior. Above the door was a colored-glass window, and the sun, shining through it, cast red and blue diamonds on the floor. Other windows were wide open.

Aunt Mercy was greeting people, everyone was, and the chatter in the church rose as more and more people arrived and took their places on the benches.

Reverend Phiri, the minister, walked onto the podium, with its wooden table and carved cross, and the hubbub slowly faded. "Dearly beloved!" He opened his arms wide.

A red bird flew in through the door, chased by a yellowy one, and darted around the podium. Sam thought it would knock into the minister, but it swooped away just in time.

When the minister finished praying, the choir, at the side of the podium dressed all in white, struck up a hymn. All joined in the chorus, then the verses, too, harmonizing, bodies swaying within the confines of the benches. Sam swayed, too, singing lustily; Amai had liked this song. The temperature rose.

They sat down again, Aunty mopping her forehead with a cloth produced from her bosom.

"Jesus looks down on us," said the minister.

"Hallelujah!" a man called from behind.

"Amen." It was Aunty.

"Yes, my brothers and sisters, Jesus is looking down on us. He is looking down on us. As we read from his Holy Word.

"But before we hear it, let us bow our heads in prayer and

remember our sins, the words that we have said that were wrong."

"Oh, yes, sweet Jesus," came from the side.

"The things we have done and should not have done."

"Amen. It is so."

"God sees what we do and what we do not do. God will not forget until we repent."

"Oh, oh, oh." A woman swayed back and forth on the bench in front of them.

"Amen." It was the man behind once more.

The church fell silent. Sam squeezed his eyes shut and folded his hands. "Ask Macdonald to say he's sorry," he prayed, "then I can forgive him. And, God, tell Amai and Atate where I am. Tell them that I'm not at home, not anymore. Tell them I'm here. Tell them." Then he remembered Aunt Mercy's request and quickly added, "And help Robbie get better." In his mind he saw the banana-colored hair again.

There was a bang on the roof, and Sam jumped. Another bang. Sam opened his eyes. No one else seemed bothered. A thud and then a bouncing and a shrieking. From outside on the path came laughter. More shrieking up on the roof, more bouncing.

Ezelina nudged him. "It's all right," she said. "It's just monkeys fighting."

Sam closed his eyes once more and let the rise and fall of the minister's voice take him away.

He felt pressure at his side. Aunt Mercy was squeezing

up more closely. "Move over." She flapped her hand at him. "Make room." The carpenter had come in and had slid onto the end of the bench next to her. Chikondi gurgled at him from Aunty's back.

Sam shuffled to the left, squeezing Ezelina in turn, then Enock and Macdonald.

"We have strayed from your path," went on the minister.

"Yea, Lord," from behind.

"The times are bad, and we wonder why."

"Why!"

"We must repent!" The minister's voice rose to a shout.

"I have sinned, I repent!"

"Dear Lord, I repent."

The shouts were coming fast and furious now. Sam listened to hear if Macdonald's was one of the voices. It wasn't.

Behind them, Mavuto leaned forward and tapped Macdonald on the shoulder.

"Sit down!" hissed Aunt Mercy, spotting Macdonald as he stood up.

But during the next hymn he slipped out with Mavuto anyway. Sam wanted to go, too. What if they were after his shoes? Would the shoes still be there when he got back? Those two were the sinners! *They* should be repenting!

He tried to push past Ezelina, but Aunt Mercy caught his sleeve and fixed him with a gimlet eye. "You are staying here with us," she said. "That Mavuto is a bad influence. You listen to the minister."

"Only have faith and you will be saved!" The minister's voice was rising. "Faith can move mountains, as the Good Book says," and he brandished the Bible high in the air.

Maybe he didn't have enough faith, Sam thought. That was it! Perhaps if he had more faith, perhaps then he would be able to feel his amai's spirit.

The minister was shouting now, and people were on their feet and singing. Sam swayed again with the music; he liked this part.

At the end, when it was all over, everyone streamed outside and milled around under the trees. The minister stood shaking hands, talking to people, no longer shouting. He even looked his normal height again.

"Mercy Mlanga," he said as she drew alongside, with Sam and the twins in tow. He clasped her hand in both of his and leaned forward confidingly. "You and the carpenter," he said quietly to her, but not so quietly that Sam didn't catch what he was saying. "I noticed you sitting together. I hear . . . marriage?"

"I'm surprised at you, Reverend, listening to gossip!" Aunt Mercy chided him. But she smiled at him before sailing on, out to the track.

Sam was stunned, and not just at her telling the minister off. He turned to see if Ezelina and Enock had heard, but they had stopped and were in a group of others, all laughing.

"Are you going to marry the carpenter?" Sam asked, looking away from them and fighting down his loneliness.

Aunt Mercy sucked her teeth and pulled him to the side of the path so as not to block the way. "No, Sam, I'm not. He'd be trouble."

"Trouble like Mavuto?" Sam asked smugly.

"No, Sam! I don't mean that at all. The carpenter is not a bad man, and he lets Mavuto sleep in his workroom. No, it would just bring trouble if I marry him. I shall not marry again. My husband's brother asked me, as is the custom. But I said no, even to him. It is better so."

"Why?"

"Oh." She sighed. "Because of the Disease. It must not spread. The government tells us not to marry again, and I think it is wise advice. Besides, I have enough men in my life, Enock, and Macdonald and Chikondi, and"—she drew him to her—"I've got you. It's quite simple. Why should I need anyone else?"

15

SAM DIPPED RESTLESSLY IN AND OUT OF SLEEP THAT NIGHT, thoughts racing round and round in his head. If only he could talk to Amai, he would be happier; if only he could talk to her, he would maybe start to fit in. But did he want to? She would help. If only he could, if only . . .

In the morning he was the first to get up after Aunt Mercy had finished saying her prayers. He was the first to put on his clothes and go to the latrine, wash at the tap outside, and roll up his mat.

Aunt Mercy smiled at him. He was relieved to see that it was a warm smile, which took up the whole of her face. Encouraged, he asked what he'd planned to ask, one of the many times he'd been awake in the night.

"Is the radio the only place to find out when someone's died?"

Aunt Mercy paused in pulling a man's undershirt over Chikondi's head. "Sometimes people put a death notice in the newspaper." The shirt fell down over the toddler and reached to his knees. She patted his bottom. "There, now. Off you go."

Chikondi lurched toward the door to go outside.

"Was Amai in the paper?"

"I don't know."

"Did you look?"

"Sammy, I have no newspaper. No."

Sam realized then for the first time that he hadn't seen anyone reading a newspaper the way Atate and Amai had. He frowned. "But if you did want to read a newspaper, where would you buy one?"

Aunt Mercy shrugged. "Ask Macdonald. He has a friend who goes every day to the boma, to the government offices, to look at a newspaper. He goes to look for work."

"To look for work?" Sam echoed. He was puzzled. What did looking for work have to do with death notices?

"He looks for work in the advertisements in the newspaper. At the boma there are newspapers that you can read."

"Will there be a newspaper for the day Amai died?"

"Mmm, maybe. Oh, I don't know, Sammy. Enough questions. Macdonald, why are you still lying there? Get up. Enock, will you build the fire? Macdonald—water, please."

"Where's the boma?" Sam persisted. He'd just had an idea. If there was a death notice in the paper and he could have it, it would be another link to Amai, and would double the power of the photograph. He glanced at Macdonald, wondering if he would answer him.

"I'll take you."

It was Ezelina.

"Really?" He hadn't noticed that she'd been listening.

"You don't know how to get there. I can show you."

*　*　*

When they walked by the hospital, there were nurses and patients at morning prayers out in the open on the verandah, singing a hymn.

"Those are the foreign doctors."

As if Sam had needed Ezelina to tell him that! Next to the director was the woman he'd seen at the bungalow window, also in a white coat. She was singing lustily, like her husband the director. Ezelina hummed along as they passed and did a little skip. "Little Robbie is getting better," she told him. "Amai just told me. She is so happy." Round the corner of the building, Sam looked up at the grass in case Brown was there, to touch his arm. It might help with the newspaper. But no one was out there yet.

"It's too early," said Ezelina.

It wasn't too early, though, for the hut on the corner to have eggs to sell, displayed in a tin bowl on the windowsill.

They passed through the tea bushes belonging to the mission, with their dark glossy leaves; past the oven where bricks were baked; and farther till the bushes thinned out. Paths snaked off the track. Ezelina turned onto one.

"Is this the way?"

"No, but I know where there's good sugar cane." She showed him a five-kwacha coin she'd been clutching. "Amai gave it to me."

The path wound round through bush and vegetable plots until it reached a cluster of huts, their mud walls newly smoothed. The second hut they came to had the usual plot of high-growing corn next to the path, and a few vegetables. Long sticks of cane were propped against a wooden fence. Ezelina laid the coin on the top of the fence and selected one of the shorter sticks. She passed it to Sam. He put it on the ground, breathed in deeply, then, concentrating, snapped it on the ground with a stamp of his foot and handed half to Ezelina. Now they each had a stick to chew on as they walked, ripping into it with their teeth, chewing and sucking its woody sweetness as they returned to the track.

Sam liked the sound of his flip-flops on the earth. When he'd seen that Ezelina had slipped on flip-flops, he'd put his on, too, and they kept soft time with each other.

The track stopped abruptly at a river. At their feet a path snaked down to the milky, muddy water. There were women in the water, laughing and chatting. You couldn't see below their waists, the water was so cloudy, but above that they were naked, washing their hair and bodies. Ezelina was already halfway down the path, so Sam had to follow.

"Ooh! A young man!" shrieked one of the women, teasing him, her breasts bobbing on the water. "Come in and join us!"

Sam felt shy all of a sudden. He didn't answer.

"No, aunty," Ezelina said as she hopped from one stepping stone to the next. "Come on, Sam."

The first woman cackled as he hopped. She lunged at him, but he was quicker on the stones than she was in the water, and he managed to evade her. The other women laughed and cheered. Once Sam reached the opposite bank, he turned to them and bowed, and they clapped.

"You go with your girlfriend, then," said the woman, and the others laughed good-naturedly as Sam and Ezelina went on, drowning out Sam's call back to them, "She's not my girl-friend, she's my cousin!"

Across the river the track led them to another village, a row of huts that stretched on either side of the track, each with a bit of ground in front. Behind most of the huts was a vegetable plot. In front, a few carefully tended flowers grew in little hollows in the earth, as they did at Aunt Mercy's. But some huts had no flowers. Their windows were boarded up, the ground in front bore no signs of being swept, and the corn in the vegetable plots was dry and straggly. Here there had been death.

Sam and Ezelina came on small graveyards at the other side of the village, and farther along, too. Most of the graves had a simple headstone, with the name and the date of death. Sam glanced at the ones near the track. None went further back than 1990.

Yet the earth smelled good, the sky was clear, there were people on the track to greet, and Mount Mandingwe stayed there on their left, standing guard over them, morning cloud starting to thicken around its peak.

They didn't talk much as they walked. The sun was much higher in the sky by the time the track did one last turn

and decanted them onto the side of the main road, newly tarmacked. There was a bend to the left, not far from them. The
road stretched in a straight line to their right, a smooth, black
ribbon.

Sam breathed in deeply, recognizing the smell of asphalt
in the heat—a town smell, even if this didn't look one bit like
town. To the left and to the right, the road itself was empty.
but off the tarmac at the sides of the road people walked along
in a steady stream, as many going one way as there were coming the other.

A truck rattled past, overflowing with its cargo of passengers, like the truck Sam had come in.

"Which way is Blantyre?" he asked Ezelina.

She pointed left. "That way." And then she added, "I
think."

The truck was driving the wrong way then, away from
town, Sam thought. "Which way to the boma?"

"Just beyond the bend."

Again Ezelina pointed left. An old red car lumbered past,
and a bicycle. Ezelina was just turning into the stream of
walkers going left when a black motorbike swung round the
corner.

"Allan!" Sam called. "Allan!" He jumped up and down
and waved, in case Allan couldn't hear through the helmet
that made his head look like a pumpkin.

But Allan had seen them. He stopped and they ran
across the road to him. *"Muli bwanje?"* they panted.

He lifted his visor. *"Ndilo bwino, kaia inu."*

"Ndilo bwino, zikomo."

"What are you two scamps doing here?"

"We're going to the boma," said Ezelina, and Sam butted in, "Can we have a ride now?"

"Now? Both of you?"

Ezelina nodded.

"What about the boma?" Allan asked. "That's not where I'm going."

"Later," Sam said airily.

"But I'm on my way to work."

They went on looking eagerly at him. Ezelina put out a hand and stroked the leather pillion seat as if it were alive.

Allan gave a bark of laughter. "All right."

Ezelina clapped her hands, and Sam grinned fit to burst

"Listen, though, and listen well," said Allan. "You! . . . What's your name?"

"Ezza, mister."

"Right. Ezza, I want you to sit up behind me and hold on tight. Samuel," he went on, as Ezelina scrambled awkwardly onto the wide seat and sat astride, "you get on behind her and hold on tight to her in turn. Both hands, right?"

They were on and holding tight as instructed. Allan put down his visor, gunned the engine, and they were on their way.

16

THEY RODE OFF, THOUGH NOT DOWN THE SMOOTH MAIN road as Sam had expected. After only a few yards, Allan turned left onto a track marked TIFFIN TEAS and they started gently climbing. There were tea bushes on either side, growing so thickly that all they could see was a low canopy of glossy dark green. The dirt road went straight up the slope. Then it turned sharp left, and they hit a stone.

Ezelina squealed but didn't let go and didn't lose her seat. Nor did Sam. He held on tight as Allan had instructed, especially now that the whole surface was bumpier. Finally, the motorbike slowed down. Allan stopped outside a couple of large buildings and killed the engine.

He raised his visor and looked back at them before he took off the whole helmet and shook his head free in the air. "Hop off." He waited till Ezelina and Sam had gotten down, then swung his leg over the motorbike to dismount, too. A ticking sound came from the engine as it began to cool.

"What, no blue shoes today?" Allan said to Sam.

Sam scowled. "They were thieved."

"But he got them back," said Ezelina quickly.

"So why aren't you wearing them?"

"Don't want to anymore," Sam muttered, though he didn't really mean it.

"If that's the case, you might as well leave them out for someone who needs them."

"That's no good," said Ezelina sensibly. "No one will take them because they're so bright. Everyone would think they'd been thieved—especially now they've been thieved once."

"Hmm." Allan glanced at the buildings and back at them. "Since you're here, how would you like to come and help me work?"

They nodded vigorously.

"You don't even know what I'll be doing!"

Sam shrugged. The tiniest of frowns creased Ezelina's forehead.

Allan laughed. "It's all right. I'm tea-tasting. That's what I'm doing today. Come along." It was the first time Sam had seen him walk, and he had an energetic, springy step. Behind him, Sam copied his walk, step-bounce, step-bounce. Ezza joined in, hand over her mouth to smother her giggles.

They step-bounced in a line along the outside of the tea factory to a room jutting out at the side and opened the door. Allan exchanged greetings with the three others in there: *"Muli bwanje."* They were all in white cotton coats. *Like the doctors at the mission,* Sam thought, keeping close to Allan's side.

"Children, Allan?" said one of the men. "Unauthorized personnel in here? That's not allowed."

"They're hardly personnel," said another. "Don't be such a stickler, Mphamvu Bwinji." The man went over to a cupboard, took out something, and advanced on them, shaking out two white coats. "Here," he said, giving Sam one and Ezelina the other. "Put these on. It's company regulations."

Mphamvu Bwinji. Sam looked closely at the first man. Was he related to his Mr. Bwinji? He didn't dare ask, the man looked so forbidding, not at all like Allan.

"And wash your hands at the sink," Allan added, "with soap." He took a white coat down from a peg, shrugged it on, and was washing his hands while Sam and Ezelina were still fumbling with the buttons of their long coats.

They hoisted up the coats and perched on high stools so they could watch. The men poured tea into the thick white cups set out in a row in front of them and tasted it. Both Ezelina and Sam giggled when the tasters rolled the liquid in their mouths and spat it out in a bowl.

"I'm glad to see that we amuse you. Here, have a cup. You must be thirsty." Allan poured some of the third sample into two cups for them. "You can drink the whole cupful, and there's no need for you to spit it out."

The man called Mphamvu Bwinji snorted and turned his back but made no further objection. Under the gaze of the other men, Sam and Ezelina glanced at each other and, in unison, raised their cups and drank.

"And? Tell us what you think," said the kind man.

The tea was hot and strong, stronger than any that Sam had ever drunk—when he'd been allowed to—with Amai. That had been sugared. This was bitter, so bitter that the insides of his mouth seemed to shrink. He wished he could spit it out. But he drank it bravely, glancing sideways at Ezelina to see how she was liking it. Her eyes were closed, though, and her expression gave nothing away.

"*Zikomo*," she said, carefully setting the cup back in its saucer. Sam noticed that she'd managed only half.

"It's good tea," Sam said perkily.

"It is, which is why we take it to the hospital for the patients. Local tea to do them good; a small luxury. Another cup?" Allan wielded the teapot. He grinned as Sam shook his head.

"No, thank you." A thought struck Sam. "People drink a lot of tea in the desert, don't they?"

"In the desert? I wouldn't know," said Allan.

"But . . ." Sam was puzzled. "But you said you'd traveled all over Malawi."

"I have. And there's no desert in Malawi."

"Oh. But Mansa Musa talks about the desert," Sam insisted. "He travels through it all the time. It's in my book."

"Mansa Musa?"

"You know, the good king of Malawi. Years and years and years ago. In the days when Malawi was called Mali."

Allan laughed. "No, Sam. Mali isn't Malawi. It's another country, way up in the north, thousands of miles away from here. Part of Mali is desert. I expect your Mansa Musa went traveling in the Sahara Desert. No, I've never been there."

"Oh." Sam felt absurdly let down. "So there are no camels here, either?"

"In Malawi? I'm afraid not, young man. You'd have to go north to find those. Ah, don't look so disappointed." He rubbed Sam's head. "Mali's still in Africa. There's nothing to stop you going there one day."

Sam didn't think he wanted to. It'd be even farther away from where Amai and Atate lay. He couldn't bear that.

"Maybe you could walk there in your blue shoes," said Ezelina. "They're strong enough."

"What?" Sam was cross now. He really didn't want to talk about his shoes. Anyway, was she serious? Did it mean she wanted to get rid of him?

But when he looked at her, she was grinning.

"It would take you months," Allan pointed out. "A motorbike would be faster! Now, let's have those coats off you." Allan hung the white coats up, led them out of the tasting room, and pointed. "Go back the way we came, then it's right along the main road for the boma, and—"

"I know the way," Ezelina interrupted, already walking off.

Sam hung back. "We're going there because I have to find

a newspaper," he confided, almost in a whisper, to Allan. "I need to see if Amai had a death notice."

"Do you?"

Sam clammed up. He didn't want to explain in case it took away any spirit power that the notice would have. If he found a notice at all, that is.

17

BACK ON THE MAIN ROAD, THEY TURNED RIGHT, INTO THE
file of walkers. No car passed, only a bicycle, heavily laden
with sacks, and a second, wobbling on buckled wheels, and
then they were there, at a collection of old buildings
arranged round a sort of square. They headed over to the
busiest-looking place, a bungalow under the trees. At the
bottom of the steps leading up to the low long verandah,
they hesitated, till Sam spotted a faded sign over the main
entrance saying DISTRICT COMMISSIONER. A large woman
huffed and puffed her way up the steps, and they followed
in her wake, along the verandah, and into an open doorway
as two men came out.

Inside the waiting room it was crowded and hot. People
squatted against the walls, waiting patiently. The lucky ones
were on benches, crammed up against each other. A name
was called, and a man got up from one end of a bench. The
fat woman spotted it and squeezed into the space he'd left,
one buttock on, one off, vigorously flapping her hand. Next
to her on the bench, a man was fanning himself with a folded
newspaper.

A newspaper! Sam looked round the room. In the corner,
there was a high, neat pile of newspapers, with a stern look-

ing man seated alongside. At a small table nearby, two young men had papers spread out in front of them and were reading intently.

Sam went and stood in front of the man guarding the papers. "May I look?"

"Why?" The man looked him up and down.

Ezelina came to stand beside him. *"Muli bwanje."* They exchanged greetings. "Please, may we look?"

The man softened. "What are you looking for?"

Ezelina nudged Sam to answer.

"Please may I see the newspaper for the sixth of June?" It was the day Amai had died. He was politer this time.

The man lifted off the top half of the pile and rifled through the next few. "Here you are." He pulled one out. "The sixth of June. Show me your hands."

Sam put them out, palms upward.

The man looked disappointed to see them so clean. "Here, then. Take it to the table."

"Help me find Amai's death notice," Sam said to Ezelina. "This is the day she died."

They turned the pages together slowly. National news, international news. "Here." Births, deaths, marriages. Sam ran his finger slowly down the death column. Amai wasn't there.

"Sam, listen. If she died on the sixth of June, would the notice be in on the sixth? Wouldn't it be the next day?"

Idiot! Sam struck his forehead. "Will you ask the man for

the next two days? Please?" he asked. "He likes you better."

She took the paper back and returned with the other two.

"You look in the eighth, I'll look in the seventh," Sam told her.

This time he knew exactly which page to turn to. There it was! Right at the bottom of the column: *Innocence Sangala, dearly beloved wife of* . . .

Sam shifted slightly till Ezelina was between him and the man, blocking him from the man's view. He took the edge of the page where the column ended between finger and thumb and, quickly, ripped it away. He'd slipped it into the pocket of his shorts before anyone saw. Except for Ezelina. "What are you doing?" she hissed.

"Shh." He made a great show of smoothing out the pages and closing the newspaper.

"Will you take them back for me? Please, Ezza," Sam said, as she seemed to hesitate.

"Did you find what you were looking for?" the man asked.

She nodded, smiling her sweetest smile, as Sam quickly picked his way through the waiting people to the door. Outside, a small plastic bag rose in the light breeze. He grabbed it, shoved it into his pocket, and was already halfway back to the road as Ezelina reached the door.

"Wait! Not so fast!" She tried to catch up, but Sam didn't slow down. He wanted to put as much distance as possible between himself and the guardian of the papers. He knew he'd done wrong—newspapers were expensive— but he wasn't going to give the piece of paper back.

They turned off the road and were once again on the track.

"Sam!"

On he walked, *flip, flop, flip* fast went his shoes, round a bend.

Ezelina put on a spurt to catch up. "Sam!" She plucked at his arm.

At last he stopped.

"Can I see what you tore out?"

Sam nodded. Just off the track was a termite hill, and he headed for it.

They scrambled onto it and perched there, and Sam took the cutting from his pocket. Carefully, he smoothed out its crumples and placed it in the palm of his hand. They read together: "Innocence Sangala, dearly beloved wife of the late Armstrong Sangala, mother of Samuel, passed over peacefully in Blantyre, on 6 June. May God rest her soul."

"I'm going to put it next to their photograph, in the frame." Sam felt he could trust Ezza, and from the look in her eyes, she seemed to understand. He slid the cutting into the plastic bag, folded the bag, and put it back in his pocket. Just in time. A drop of water splashed onto the back of his hand. He hadn't even noticed the dark clouds gathering.

They hopped down from the hill and set off again. Rain thudded down on their bare heads. It trickled down their necks, reached their waists, and trickled on till they were soaked through. Their feet slipped wetly inside their flip-flops, so they took them off and carried them. Soft mud churned up between their toes and squelched as they walked.

Sam laughed. It could rain all it liked, he didn't care. His cutting was safe, inside the plastic bag.

The rain stopped just as they came to the river, and the sun came out as if it had never been away. They half-clambered, half-slid down the path, muddy now, crossed the water, jumping from one stepping stone to another, and climbed up the other side, holding tree roots to keep them from slipping. Back on the track, steam rose up and with it the thick, dark red smell of the earth. Steam rose from their clothes, too, as they began to dry out in the warmth of the sun. Sam reckoned he'd walked at least three hours that day, and they weren't even in sight of the mission yet. He wasn't used to walking like this. "At home," he told Ezelina, "we had a car. Amai used to drive me to school in it. And to other places, too."

"We should get firewood," said Ezelina.

"The wood'll be wet."

"It'll dry."

"Well, then, when I got back from school," Sam plunged on, "I played games on my computer. Have you ever seen a computer, Ezza?"

She shook her head.

"Never mind, I expect you will one day," he said grandly. "Anyway, in one of the games, there are these aliens, only they're not really aliens, they're humans who left Earth hundreds of years before and since then they've changed. They come back to Earth and try to capture as many Earthmen as they can, to experiment on, and you have to stop them getting round!"

"Let's get the sticks here," said Ezelina.

"Oh. All right. Anyway, you have to keep them from getting to the main control tower, because if they get there . . ."

He was talking to himself. Ezelina was yards away already, looking for firewood. "Ezza?" he said. "I want to tell you what happens next—in the game, I mean."

She didn't answer. All right, then, if she wasn't interested, neither was he. Why should he pick up sticks, anyway? They'd collected a lot only the day before, hadn't they?

Above her back, as she crouched over, Sam saw a tall hedge in the distance that he thought he recognized. He turned round. There were the straggling trees on a knoll to his left, and Mount Mandingwe guarding him. So the graveyard where the twins' atate was buried wasn't far away.

He was right. It was the enormous hedge Enock had warned him about. "We," Enock had said. It was forbidden to "we." "We" from the village. Sam wasn't from the village, was he? He was from Blantyre. And he was curious.

He glanced back over his shoulder. Ezelina wasn't

watching. He crossed the ground toward the high hedge and prowled down alongside.

The hedge stopped abruptly and turned at a right angle in a line. He followed that line. It, too, ended and turned, and then turned another corner. He went all the way round. Four sides. He saw no opening. But the hedged-in area was so large, he knew there had to be something inside; it couldn't be solid. And that, in turn, meant that there had to be an entrance.

He glanced back. In the distance Ezelina looked quite small, sitting on a stone with her back to him. Quietly, he retraced his steps, out of her sight, walking more slowly this time, examining the green barrier, thick and dense and dark.

There!

He had been looking for a gap in the hedge, maybe with a gate. He hadn't been looking for a hole. But that was what he found. It was as if the bottom quarter of the hedge had been torn open. The hole wasn't very wide, but it was wide enough for a grownup to get through, and high enough, too, if he bent. Even Sam had to duck a little in order to enter.

The air rushed out of him as he was knocked to the ground.

"Don't do it!" Ezelina stood over him. "You mustn't go there! Didn't you hear me calling?"

Sam shook his head, startled by her attack. From where he lay on the ground, he had just a glimpse through the hole. It looked as if it opened up inside. He could see shady green light. He could feel a great stillness. It seemed to be beckoning him. He began to wriggle nearer.

"Get up!" Ezelina sounded so fierce that he scrambled to his feet at once.

"Why can't I go through?"

"Because you'll be cursed. Your eyes'll drop out for seeing, your ears will block for hearing, your mouth will never open."

He stared at her. He looked back at the hedge. "How do you know?"

"Oh!" She was exasperated. "Can't you even feel it?"

And he could. He could feel something, but it was calling to him, not pushing him away. "Is it where the nchimi lives?"

She tossed her head. "You've got to come, you can't stay here. I can't stay here. We're not old enough yet. Come away. Here, take these." She thrust a bundle of sticks at him, put another on her head, and started off.

"Slow down, Ezza!" Sam called, hurrying to catch up. She was almost running. "Anyone'd think you were scared."

"I am scared." Her eyes were blazing. "You should be, too. That place isn't for us."

18

By the time they got back to Aunty's, the rain there had stopped, and the mud of the track steamed gently in the clear sun. They had hardly spoken a word to each other the rest of the way.

Now Sam went straight indoors. He took out the cutting and folded the torn edges till it looked neat, then he squeezed one side into the frame. It covered his mother's feet, but somehow that didn't matter.

"What are you doing?" It was Macdonald.

"He's putting his mother's death notice from the paper into his parents' photograph," Ezelina explained, "to bring her closer."

"How could you!" Sam looked daggers at Ezelina. He hadn't wanted anyone else to know, and Macdonald least of all.

"What?" Ezelina asked. "What have I said?" She looked hurt.

Sam turned away. She had spoiled it! If you talked about a thing with power, that made it weaker. Macdonald would have seen the cutting eventually, but Sam wished he hadn't seen it so soon, and he wouldn't have known what it meant.

Sam had thought Ezelina was his friend, that he could trust her with his secret.

He sat on the floor with his back to the wall, knees drawn up to his chest, arms round his knees, his head down. Someone touched his hair, but he ignored Ezelina— he supposed it was she—and he felt her move away.

At last he sensed that he was alone. He looked up at the photograph and the cutting, but it was difficult to see them properly because his eyes were wet, so Amai and Atate looked blurred. Even so, he willed Amai's spirit to be there somewhere in the photograph and the paper. If only she could be, he'd feel less strange in this place. Aunt Mercy had said he'd get used to being here, but it had been days now, and still he didn't feel it was home.

Where was Amai's spirit?

He reached over to his case, flipped open the lid, and took out his precious running shoes. He sniffed their familiar smell. He frowned at the new grass stain and the smudges of soot and the caked mud. He rubbed off the mud, but the other marks wouldn't come out. He put the shoes on anyway, in the hope that they would help. At least they were a link with Amai.

He swallowed back snot, wiped his eyes, went to the shelf for *Mansa Musa,* and took the book to the table. Before Kankan Musa had become the Mansa, the ruler, he'd been alone, too; he'd gone searching, too, for his father. He would have known what it was like for Sam now, searching for his mother.

"You claim to be a man but have not yet mastered . . ."

The words swam in front of his eyes, and a teardrop fell onto the "yet," magnifying it. He dabbed at it with the bottom of his shirt, but more tears were falling. It was no good, he couldn't read just at the moment, not on his own, not without Amai. He wanted to be playing with his friends in town, he wanted to run home and find Amai sitting in her usual place waiting for him, he wanted to be in his own bed in his own bedroom.

Sam slammed the book shut, rubbed his wet eyes hard with the back of his hand, put the book back on the shelf. Then he took it down again and went outside. Ezelina called out, but he brushed past her, hiding the book. Aunt Mercy had said it had to stay on the shelf. But it was his book, he could do what he wanted with it. "I'm going to see Brown," he said over his shoulder, walking away fast.

"I'll come with you." She ran to catch up and walked fast alongside him, but he didn't even glance at her, and she let him go on ahead. "Come back soon." Her voice trailed into the air behind him.

Outside the hospital Sam went up the grassy slope, looking. There were patients outside, some sitting, some lying down, some on a cloth, some just on the grass. There were children, and there were guardians. But there was no Brown, and no Stella. There were men as skinny as sticks, there were women coughing and spitting, but none of them was Brown.

On the verandah opposite he noticed a group of men, gesticulating and exclaiming in alarm. The Danish doctor was there among them, silent, listening.

He caught sight of Sam. "Hey! You!" The director was beckoning.

Sam pointed to himself. "Me?"

The director nodded. "Would you come here, please?"

Sam went round the verandah and stood in front of the foreign doctor. He smiled, wondering if the doctor was going to ask him to help with the computer.

"Is this the boy?" the doctor asked one of the men.

"It is." The man wasn't smiling.

The foreigner bent down to him. "Have you taken the laptop?"

Sam was stunned. This wasn't what he'd expected.

"Did you take the laptop?" the doctor repeated.

"No." Sam shook his head. "Of course not."

"It has been stolen."

"Not by me! Why do you accuse me?" Sam cried wildly.

"No one is accusing you." The doctor was stern. "But you were seen leaving the computer room yesterday. And you know how to use it."

"That doesn't make the lad a thief," remonstrated one of the other men. "I have been hearing about him."

"Where is Mr. Bwinji?" Sam couldn't see him in the small group. "He will tell you I'm not a thief!"

"Mr. Bwinji isn't here. He had to go back to his own village, to a funeral," the first man answered. "We do not know when he will return."

"Look," said the director impatiently. "We *have* to find that laptop. I want a full search. Perhaps we should start by talking to this young man's mother."

"He is living with Mercy," said the man who'd stuck up for Sam.

"Mercy Mlanga?" The director looked surprised. "Is it you who's just come here to live? Her nephew?"

Sam nodded.

"Then I shall have a word with Mrs. Mlanga myself." He tugged at his ear.

"*She* hasn't taken it!" Sam was quite sure of that.

"You may go." The doctor dismissed him.

His heart knocking against his ribs, Sam jumped down to the ground and ran along the path round to the next wing of the hospital. He looked in at the first ward, hunting for Brown. Ten iron bedsteads, ten men lying there, most of them under a sheet or cloth. He went to the open doorway and entered. The ward was very quiet. A couple of the men turned their heads wearily to see who had come in.

Sam smiled uncertainly at them and walked down the rows of beds. He found Brown lying in the far corner, his eyes closed.

Sam knelt down at the side of the bed and reached out. Before he could touch the stump, Brown opened his eyes.

"Hello, young man. Have you come to get some luck again?"

Sam shrugged. Of course he had. But if he said so, tears might come, and he didn't want that. Also if he said they thought he was a thief. "Look." He produced *The Travels of Mansa Musa*. He'd been going to show it only to Brown, but now that everything was so wrong and Brown was so ill, it seemed a good idea to read to him. He'd read to Amai near the end, after she'd stopped being able to read to him.

He opened the book, told Brown the title, and began to read, haltingly at first, but then with more confidence as he saw the small smile on Brown's face.

"Thank you." From the way Brown said it a while later, Sam knew he'd heard enough for the time being. Sam wished he could have gone on. While he'd been reading, his troubles had seemed to vanish. "Help me to sit up."

Sam stood. He raised Brown a little, just as he used to do for Amai. The movement made Brown cough. The cough was so great it seemed that his fragile body would shatter. When it was over, he fought for breath. Then he turned his head back to Sam and held out his stump. "Here."

Sam touched it. He stayed like that, his hand on the stump, and Brown didn't pull it away. It was strangely comforting.

"Tell me," Brown ordered in a hoarse whisper, so as not

to set the coughing off again. "What's up? Why have you really come to see me, and on your own?"

Sam wasn't sure where to start, there was so much to tell. "I have no friends . . ." He halted. Ezza'd been kind to him— but she'd told Macdonald about the cutting. And what about Enock? But . . . "Macdonald hates me," he went on, "and I hate him, too. He reads my book. He stole my running shoes. Amai gave them to me."

Brown sighed. "Count your blessings, my boy. Have you not food to eat? Shelter above your head? Family to look after you?"

Yes, thought Sam, *but it's not home.*

"Does the sun shine? Is there someone to hug you?"

Yes, thought Sam, *but Aunty isn't Amai.* "I want Amai!" he wailed. "And I can't talk to her. It's all wrong. She's been buried wrong. It's that Mr. Gunya—it's his fault," though he knew that wasn't so; it had been his mother's wish. "She should have been buried here with our ancestors, where she was born, and now I can't feel her near me and there's no grave here where I can go and speak to her."

Brown was so still that Sam began to think he hadn't heard him, maybe hadn't even been listening.

"And they think I've stolen a computer, the laptop. And I haven't. They're going to do a search. It's not fair! No one bothered searching anywhere when my shoes were taken!"

Brown closed his eyes.

Perhaps Sam's instinct about coming had been wrong.

But then Brown spoke, his eyes still closed. "Listen carefully, young man. You have to make a sacrifice. What is precious to you, you must give away. And when you have given them away, you must speak no more of them. Those blue shoes . . ." He paused to catch his breath.

Sam looked down at them. With his free hand he reached down and stroked the cool leather.

"Give them away. They are only things. They bring you trouble. Let another wear them."

Sam was so shocked, he took his hand off Brown's stump.

149

19

AUNT MERCY WAS THERE WHEN HE GOT BACK. SHE WAS speaking to Mavuto—and the others were standing close, listening. Sam put the book behind his back so she wouldn't see it.

"Why not?" Mavuto said, scowling.

"I've explained already," Aunt Mercy said. "You are fifteen years old. That is old enough to look after yourself."

"I am trying!" Mavuto cried. "But still, why won't you let me stay?"

"What is wrong with sleeping at the carpenter's?"

"He doesn't cook for me. If you married him . . ."

The twins looked at each other uneasily. "Marry?" asked Ezelina.

"Marry?" echoed Enock.

"Hasn't she told you?" Mavuto turned to them. "He wants them to marry, and then we'd all live together."

"But I am not going to marry him." Aunt Mercy was calm. "Even though he is a good man."

"And a good storyteller," Macdonald broke in.

"I am not going to marry again," Aunt Mercy went on, as if he hadn't interrupted. "It is better that way."

"But it would help," Mavuto pleaded. "If the doctors'

children died, you would lose your job. And then you would need money."

There was a shocked silence.

"Amai, you said Robbie was getting better," Ezelina said.

"And so he is. Mavuto, it is kind of you to be concerned, but I manage, thank you. And my job is not at risk."

"If you manage, why can I not come and live here, too? Like Sam has?" He threw Sam a small, unhappy smile.

"We have no more room."

"It's because of Sam that we have no room!" cried Macdonald.

"That is enough! Mavuto and Macdonald, you will please go to the market and fetch beans as relish for tonight's supper. Mavuto, you are welcome to eat with us tonight, but I will have no more talk of marriage, or of you living here." She glared at them both.

She turned to Sam. "Will you sweep the yard? It needs it. Ezelina, will you fetch the matches?"

There! Sam himself was just trouble, he felt sure of it. If he hadn't been there, Aunt Mercy would have taken in Mavuto.

He slouched indoors for the broom and put the book back on the shelf, his heart heavy. No one really wanted him. Some even thought he was a thief, no better than Macdonald. He was bringing shame on Aunt Mercy. Perhaps Brown's advice had been good. Perhaps if he sacrificed the shoes, something would turn out right.

He sat on the floor and took off the shoes. "I'm sorry, Amai," he said, looking up at the photograph, just in case. Then he went out and swept the yard, marking the earth with the best arcs he could manage, thinking furiously all the while.

He returned the broom to its nail in the wall, picked up the shoes, and walked barefoot round the back, skirting the latrine, not wanting Ezelina or Enock to ask what he was doing. He halted and hid the shoes under his shirt before walking purposefully onto the soccer field. No one was playing. Good.

He went to the far goalpost, set the shoes down where he had left them that other time, and walked away.

But before he had turned the corner at the market, he heard the *slap, slap* of bare feet running behind. "Sam! Sam! Here, you forgot your shoes." One of Enock's friends was holding them out to him.

"Oh. Thanks," he said.

"That's okay. See you later."

Sam nodded. He stood there, irresolute, till the other boy was out of sight. Then he bent down and put the shoes in the middle of the track.

"Don't leave your shoes there!" A tiny girl was looking up at him. "Your amai will be cross with you." Quickly, she stuck her thumb in her mouth.

"Thanks," he said. He picked them up again. He walked on a bit, round the corner to where fewer people seemed to be passing. There was a flat stone on the right. He put the shoes down on the stone and walked away.

"Samuel!" came a call from behind.

He paused and turned.

It was the minister. "I think these are yours." He held the shoes out to Sam. "You must take better care of your possessions, or someone might steal them."

Sam muttered "Thank you" and took the shoes. There had to be some other way of sacrificing them. This way just wasn't working.

20

SAM WOKE UP EARLY THE NEXT MORNING. HE WAS uneasy. Supper had felt different. The carpenter hadn't come and told stories afterward, and Aunt Mercy had seemed thoughtful and had not talked much. So all evening they'd been quiet, too. She said that the Danish doctor had been asking her questions—and she'd glanced at Sam but hadn't said any more than that. Before rolling out his mat and lying down, Sam had touched the newspaper cutting and his mother's shoulder in the photograph with his fingertip. Ezelina and Enock looked away quickly when he turned and saw them watching.

He knew what he must do. When Aunty left for the doctors', taking Chikondi with her, Macdonald went with Mavuto, and Ezelina and Enock wandered off he didn't know where, though Ezza had asked him if he wanted to go with them. When they had all left, Sam went to his case, took out his shirt, and spread it out on the table. He walked to the door just to check that no one was coming. Then he took down his two books from the shelf, *Oliver Twist* and *The Travels of Mansa Musa,* and put them on the shirt, along with his Game Boy, which he rescued from the end of the bed where Enock had left it after trying to play with it earlier. He flicked it on. Nothing happened. He pressed the button again, shook it. Still nothing. Enock must have played with it for so long that all the electricity in it was gone. Sam flung it back on the bed; it was useless now.

He reached up for the photograph and the cutting and put them on the pile. Then he thought for a moment. It wouldn't do to let the others find out too soon that he had gone. Anyway, the photograph didn't seem to be working. He left it on the table and pressed his fists hard into his eyes—there was no time for tears.

Sam sat on the floor and put on his blue shoes, brushing them first with his hand. He tied the corners of his shirt together around his things, then untied them, picked up the box of matches, and put that in, too—you never knew when matches might come in handy. He retied the shirt so that it was a bag. Looping the knot around his fingers, he slung his shirt-bag over his shoulder and left the hut, going round the back by the latrine. Sam walked calmly, as if nothing was up, past the hospital, past the egg hut. He reached the edge of the mission settlement, and still no one had called to him to come back. *You see?* he said to himself. *No one really wants you, or else someone would have noticed.* He ran then. He jumped over the hollows that the rain had carved out in the baked mud of the track.

He slowed to a more respectful walk as he passed the graveyard under the trees. Not just because it was where Enock and Ezza's father was buried, but also because there was a group of men sitting talking, mourning near the fresh mound of a grave. Once past the last grave of the graveyard, he ran again.

He came to a termite hill and leaned against it to ease the stitch in his side and catch his breath. There were puffs of cloud in the bright blue sky, but the air was so still, a feather would fall straight to earth if you dropped it. Not that he had a feather to drop. He had nothing. *Not quite true,* he thought, imagining Brown telling him so. He was lucky to be wearing a T-shirt that had no holes, lucky to have a pair of shorts that were still tough, not at all threadbare. *Lucky!* He snorted.

He pushed himself away from the termite hill. A cyclist bumped along a track on the other side, and he crouched down, not wanting to be seen. Word got around so quickly. Still crouching, he looked to the side. Mount Mandingwe loomed there, high, flat-topped, imposing, the landmark Ezza had told him to use as a guide. *Keep it on your right and you'll find your way back to the mission,* she had said. It was on his left now.

He didn't want to find his way back. He was leaving. But first there was something he had to do.

The cyclist was out of sight. Sam stood up straight again and headed off, away from the path. He didn't want anyone to know where he was going. If he went left from the main track and walked a bit, then went right and right again, he should come out more or less at the place he was heading for.

He came on a small compound of family huts, and

chickens scattered, squawking, as he disturbed their peck-ing. He skirted the compound, and the path forked. One path was straight ahead; the other meandered to the left. There was none to the right. He scratched his head in bewil-derment, then decided to go straight ahead.

That path eventually led him to another cluster of huts. Long sticks of cut sugar cane were propped up against a fence, but he had no coin in his pocket. He even checked to make sure. He had no food with him at all.

A woman came round her hut and saw him standing there. He quickly greeted her. *"Muli bwanje?"*

"Ndili bwino, kaia inu," she answered.

"Ndili bwino, zikomo," he replied mechanically, gazing at the sugar cane, wondering how he could get a piece without money.

It was easy. The woman smiled, following his gaze. She gave him a short piece of sugar cane that had broken off. "Here," she said. "Going far?"

He didn't answer, just smiled at her in thanks.

"Cat got your tongue?"

He tried to think what to answer, but she turned away impatiently. "Off you go, then!"

He needed no second telling. He bit into the sugar cane. Chewing and sucking on it, he carried on, came to another fork. Was it left or right that he should be going now? *Where . . . is . . . it? Where . . . are . . . you?* he found him-self saying with every step he took. On he went, *Where . . .*

is . . . it?, till the trees around him thinned, and ahead of him he saw space. He took the sugar cane from his lips and stayed absolutely still. Then he hurried—and, yes, there was a track. He stepped out onto it and looked around. For the moment, there was no one.

He was where he wanted to be! There, on the other side, the far side of the field, was that tall hedge. He walked fast, going round the edge of the field till he reached the hedge, and then round the back of the hedge till he came to the low opening.

He stopped. He turned to check that no one was around, that no one was there to see him. He listened to make sure there was no one approaching. He took his shirt-bag off his shoulder and stuck the uneaten part of the sugar cane inside it. Clutching the bundle to his chest so that it wouldn't catch on the twigs and thorns, he looked round once more.

Then he ducked and went inside.

21

ONCE ON THE OTHER SIDE OF THE OPENING, SAM straightened up and gazed. He was in a great space, bigger even than the mission church, as big as a cathedral. But this was no cathedral. The ground was dark green, except in the black corners where no sun reached. Neither the grass nor the small plants on the ground grew any higher than his knee.

No breeze blew the grass and leaves, no bird sang, no insect whirred its wings. The great space was deserted. No one greeted him. The place was half-dead, and yet it felt half-alive. It was hot and close. He looked up high, where the hedges turned into trees, and the trees grew so thickly and densely that their branches met and crossed over his head. He was alone. But he could sense something, something powerful, something *other*. The other days when he'd felt it somehow beckoning to him, he'd thought that it could be a place of safety. Now he was not quite so sure.

He took one step forward and another, and a third.

He whirled round, heart thudding.

There was no one to be seen. There was no one and nothing, not behind him, not to the side, nor to the front when he turned back to the safety of the hedge, the thick green growing wall. And yet there was a presence. It was as if he could feel the pulsing of a great heart. He didn't know if it was good or evil. If he stayed there, not moving, he sensed that the something might grow over him and smother him. *Your eyes will drop out for seeing, your ears will block for hearing, your mouth will never open.* Ezza's warning rang through his head as if she was beside him and speaking. But he had to stay inside now, he had to stay until he had done what he had come to do.

He put down his shirt-bag and stepped forward once more, moving gently and cautiously. He didn't want to awaken anything.

He stopped, his mouth dry. *Where had that thought come from?*

He forced himself to go on. Ahead of him, close now, he could see a large, flat stone. He would use that for his sacrifice. Perhaps it had been used for that before, another voice said in his mind. He shuddered.

He reached the stone. Still nothing moved. His back prickled. He must not turn round and look to check, not until he had made his sacrifice. He sat down, and in his nervousness he overbalanced clumsily. He righted himself. Swiftly, he undid his shoes. He stood then and held them out gravely, one in the palm of each hand, toes pointing toward the stone. Blue running shoes, Amai's last gift to him.

"Please tell my ancestors where Amai is buried," he whispered, barely moving his lips, not knowing to whom or what he was whispering. He laid the shoes down, left one first, then the right one, in the center of the blank stone. "And please tell Amai where to find me. Please tell her that I am in Mandingwe—that I am in the village where she was born."

He waited. He didn't know what he was waiting for. A sign, maybe.

His scalp crawled. His skin turned cold and clammy. He almost could not breathe.

He shouldn't be here! Enock had told him so. Ezza had told him so. What would Brown say if he knew where he'd gone?

Out! Get out! a silent voice shouted in his head.

In that second he whipped round and blundered away from the stone, desperately trying not to make a noise. He picked up his bundle where he'd dropped it and gasped. There, on the ground, were bones, three of them, crossed in a funny sort of pile. He shuddered. Gathering his bundle close to his chest, he backed away, facing the cavernous green space.

Nothing. Nothingness. A great, powerful nothingness that would help him. His heart beat so hard, his blood rushed so noisily in his ears, he knew he could be heard, he knew that something knew he was there. Or was it a great powerful nothingness that would come for him if he didn't get out? Now!

Back. He stumbled and fell. Something jabbed his cheek. A pointy stick, low in the ground. He put his hand to his cheek and it came away bloody. He grabbed his bundle, which had fallen beside the stick, and got unsteadily to his feet, keeping his eyes fixed on the great big space, making sure that nothing was about to come rushing out of it toward him. "O powerful tokolosh, O powerful spirit, let me go. I honor you." The prayer had risen unbidden to his lips.

He inched backward. He jumped as something stuck in his back. It was twigs! He had reached the hedge!

He turned. Where was the gap? He went to the left. He looked back over his shoulder. Nothing. Farther to the left. No gap. Sobbing, he went to the right, farther along, farther. Where was the opening? Faster, almost running now, he beat against the hedge with his hands in panic, desperate to find where the growth thinned, no longer looking back. *Hurry! Hurry!*

"Amai!" he cried. The cry tore out of him, all the way from the depths of his belly. *"Amai!"*

There, suddenly, to his side, a shimmer of light. He raced to it. It was the gap. Sobbing, he ducked under and came out the other side, back in the field.

He ran and ran, not looking where he was going, up a slope, down into a dip, till the stitch in his side stabbed him too hard to go on. He stopped, panting, and turned to look. He could no longer see the tall, dark hedge; it was hidden from sight. There was no path or track that he could see, either.

He staggered over to a tree, dropped to the ground on his back, and closed his eyes. If anything was coming for him now, he didn't want to see it. "Amai," he whispered.

He heard birdsong. He opened his eyes and stared at the sky. Right above him, a bird was trilling as it flew. Something tickled his arm. Carefully, he rolled his eyes and turned his head just slightly. It was a blade of grass, bowing in the breeze. He looked at it in wonder. He raised his head. There was Mount Mandingwe with its cloud cover. He was safe.

22

Sam sat up and pulled his bag to him. He wanted sugar cane.

It wasn't there.

It must have dropped out along the way. Or fallen in the secret place.

But he was thirsty. He badly needed it to suck on.

He wouldn't go back for it. No way. He couldn't. That place had not been a refuge. He had to travel on.

He shuffled over to the tree and leaned against it. It was only then that he felt how much his feet were stinging. He examined them. They were cut, and he could see the black ends of thorns. He hadn't been looking where he'd run. He licked his finger and touched his cheek, then looked at the finger. There was blood on it, but dried blood. He licked it again and gently rubbed his cheek until finally the finger came away clean and he no longer tasted the rusty saltiness of his blood.

It took him longer to pull out all the thorns from his feet as the sun climbed higher and higher in the sky. Once they were out, he wet his finger with spit and ran it over the cuts.

He leaned back and closed his eyes.

The sun reached its height and began its slow descent. Sam sat there, not moving.

At last he got up. He slung his bundle over his shoulder and made his way, stumbling a little, across the rough land, trying not to wince when he trod on a cut. He didn't know where he was going. He was so thirsty, so hungry.

He reached a field of corn. A narrow path threaded its way down the middle of the tall plants. For the first time he wondered if Amai had walked here, right on this spot, when she was growing up.

There was a gleam ahead of him. Again. The sunshine was catching something that glittered. Water! Sam's spirits lifted, and he started walking more quickly.

It wasn't water.

He broke into a stumbling run. Hard leaves slapped his arms, but he didn't care. It was something black and gleaming. It was the motorbike, Allan Poot's motorbike.

Sam came out on a narrow track where the bike was standing. He touched it. It was warm under his fingers, but was that the warmth from the sun, or because the engine had recently been turned off? There was no ticking sound as there had been before, but perhaps that didn't mean anything.

He looked round. There was no sign of Allan, only the corn plants, on the other side of the track, too. He didn't know where exactly he was going, searching for Amai, but a motorbike might get him there more quickly.

Sam thought he could remember how the machine

worked. He clambered aboard. The pedals were a bit low for him, but by standing, he could reach them. *Now,* he thought, *left hand accelerator, right hand clutch, wrist-twist action.* He did so.

Nothing happened. He was wrong. He tried again. Right hand accelerator, left hand clutch.

No sound came from the machine. He kicked down on the pedal.

It was no use. He'd forgotten you needed a key to turn it on. Allan had done that first, he remembered now.

He slumped back on the broad leather seat, dropped his head on his arms, stretched out over the handlebars, and wept.

23

SOMEONE WAS GENTLY SHAKING SAM'S SHOULDER. HE looked up blearily.

It was Allan. "Where did you spring from, young Samuel? I go away for just a moment to relieve myself, and when I come back, I find you."

Sam lifted his arm to point in the direction of the hedge, and let it drop again. "I came through the corn," he said. "Please, have you got any water?"

Allan opened the container behind the motorbike seat, took out a bottle, and passed it to him. "Thirsty, eh?" he said as Sam gulped at it. His eyes moved to Sam's feet. "They're bleeding," he said, pointing. "Maybe you should have worn shoes coming through the corn."

Sam didn't respond. Carefully, he screwed the top back on the bottle.

"Where are those shoes of yours? Have you lost them?"

Sam shook his head, avoiding Allan's gaze. *You must speak no more of them,* Brown had cautioned him.

"Hmm." Allan considered him, head to one side. "Is this yours?" He picked up the shirt-bag, lying in the dirt. "You're not very talkative today, are you?" he commented when Sam still didn't answer.

Allan weighed the bundle in his hand, felt it, and frowned. "Were you running away?" he asked suddenly. "Is that it? Eh?"

He waited until, at last, a small "yes" came from Sam.

"And did you think the motorbike would help you?"

Sam glanced up at him, relieved that he didn't sound crosser. "You told me Mansa Musa came from the Sahara Desert. It'd be quicker getting there by motorbike."

"Did I? Is that where you were going? To see Mansa Musa?"

Sam slumped again. He shook his head. "Mansa Musa's dead. I think he died a long time ago."

"And in Mali," Allan said. "So where were you really going, young man?"

"I want to find Amai. She's not here. She should have been buried here, it's all wrong that she isn't. I can't talk to her. Mansa Musa went looking in the desert for his father, to talk to him. If I could talk to her, it would be all right."

"And you thought you could do the same."

"I went inside the high hedge." The words rushed out before Sam could stop them. He clapped his hand to his mouth so that no more could come out. Ezza had told him the curse. He looked appealingly at Allan.

"The high hedge," Allan repeated quietly. He stared at Sam, not blinking. "Over there, through the corn?

"Sometimes," he went on, speaking slowly and fixing Sam with his eyes, "sometimes there are things you must not speak of, because they are sacred. Things that perhaps I have heard of. Things," he said, "that are not for you because you are too young. I shall not speak of them, either."

Sam stared back at him. The two of them stayed like that. It was as if, Sam thought, as if Allan was testing him in some way.

Allan broke the silence. He opened the storage compartment at the back of his motorbike. "Here." He passed Sam his bundle. "Put it in."

But there was something in there already, at the bottom, something smooth, hard, and black. Sam paused. "What's that?"

"What? Oh, I see. A laptop."

"Is it yours?" Sam stared at Allan, this man with his sticking-out ears and paler skin, an awful suspicion in his mind.

Allan shook his head. "It's someone else's."

Sam felt a rush of fury. He flung himself at Allan, beating his chest with his fists. "You took it! And you didn't tell anyone!"

"Now, wait a minute." Allan grabbed Sam's fists and held them tightly. "I haven't taken anything. Mphamvu Bwinji's brother brought it to him. He wanted to get onto the Internet. He said that he'd heard that we could do it from our telephone connection at the tea factory. But it's no good; the thing needs a modem. I said I'd bring it back, along with more tea for the hospital. I meant to yesterday, but I couldn't get away. How come you know about the laptop?"

"They think it's stolen! They said I'm the thief, but I'm not, I'm not!"

"Of course you're not a thief. Now, come on, enough of this. I'm not a thief, and you're not a thief. Nor is Mphamvu Bwinji's brother; he was borrowing it, that's all. Put your bundle in. The sooner we get back to the mission, the better," Allan said. "I'm taking you home."

"I haven't got a home!" Sam burst out. "Macdonald hates me, and Mavuto wants to live there but he can't because I'm there, so *he* hates me, and Enock doesn't really like me because he likes Macdonald, and he told me not to go to—" He stopped quickly. "And Ezza's only being kind because she has to be. I hate them, too."

Allan looked thoughtfully at Sam. "Do you hate them, really? I rather liked Ezelina, and I thought you did. You seemed to when I met you the other day."

"She's all right," Sam muttered. "I suppose."

"And what about your aunt? Aunt Mercy, isn't it?"

"She's just . . ."

Allan waited to see if Sam was going to say any more. When he didn't, he pointed to the motorbike. "Come on, young Samuel, up you get."

Sam wanted to argue, but he didn't dare. Allan sounded so firm.

Allan put on his helmet, swung his leg over the motor-bike, and got on in front of Sam.

"I'm not Samuel!" Sam shouted suddenly at his back.

Allan twisted round. "Oh, aren't you? I rather thought you were."

Sam shook his head. "My name's Sam."

"Right you are. Sam it is."

Allan stuck his thumb in the air. He turned the key in the ignition, twist, twist, left, right, pressed the pedal, and they were off in a swirl of dust.

24

ON THE TRACK BEHIND THE DOCTORS' HOUSE, ALLAN stopped and killed the engine, and dismounted. Sam slid off, surprised. Before Allan had even removed his helmet, four boys around Sam's age came running up. Allan took the key from the ignition, tossed it in the air, and pocketed it. Two more boys arrived, and a girl. "You may sit on the bike while we are gone," he told them, "but be careful with it, understand? Guard it for me. We shall be back soon."

He put the helmet on the head of one of the boys, strapping it on and closing the visor. "You look after that for me, too. Come on, Samuel."

Sam stamped his foot. "Sam!" he said.

Allan looked coolly at him. "Sam. Sorry. Come on, then."

Allan led Sam off onto a path. It climbed gradually, and then more steeply, through long grass and low twigs that brushed Sam's bare legs as he passed. It wound round fallen branches and a tree and went on higher, till at last they came out on a ridge. The mission was far behind them.

Allan sat down and patted the ground beside him. "Sit, sit."

Sam sat in the long grass, not knowing why he was there and too tired to ask. The grass waved in the sluggish breeze, tickling his knees.

Allan spoke at last. "I want to tell you something. My amai died when I was the same age as you."

"Oh." Sam nibbled his finger and thought for a moment. "Were you there?" he asked tentatively.

"I was. Like you. But she didn't die in bed. It was a car crash. I was thrown out of the window into a field and I was saved. But Amai was killed. It happened when they tried to pick her up. That was the moment she died. I saw the life in her go." Allan's words rose above the loud chirruping of the crickets. Sam thought back to when he had seen the life leave Amai, vanishing into the air.

173

Allan went on slowly. "I thought my heart would break. It was when we were in Holland. That's where she's buried, not here. I used to go to her grave and talk to her."

Sam looked straight ahead at the sky.

"At night I lay awake, wondering where she had gone. But my father used to look at me, and he would tell me that he could see my amai in me. He said I was carrying her in me."

Down below, way ahead, stretched a flat expanse of land. Far in the distance was an uneven line of hills, like a smudge in the sky. Just above them the sun was starting to sink. As the deep red orb slipped down and touched the smudge, rays of orange, pink, and purple shot out into the sky.

At Sam's side, Allan sighed deeply. "Look out there," he said. "Look at the world. We think we are important. Whenever my troubles seem too great, I come to a place like this and look out. It makes me see how we are just part of a vast world."

Fingers of lavender and yellow streaked across the plain, catching the sparkle of water in a river, highlighting a clump of trees here, a cluster of huts there.

"When I came back to our country with my father," Allan went on, "I worried about leaving Amai behind. But, you know, even though I couldn't go to her grave, I was still able to talk to her."

Down below, blue smoke spiraled up from cooking fires as people began to prepare their evening meal. The sun dipped behind the hills, making them stand out black against the deep purple and red sky.

"I used to get away to a quiet place, a place like this. And when I was in a quiet place, I could talk to her and feel that she was listening."

A dog barked in the distance, and another answered. Their barks intermingled, as if in conversation.

Sam looked up at the sky. *Amai?* he called in his mind, trying it.

"You see, Sam," Allan went on, "when we die, we aren't just left in the earth. We go to heaven. Which doesn't mean that we go away. It means that instead of being only there in the earth, we're everywhere. We're where the people we love want us to be when they think of us. And we're in the people whom we have loved, who have memories of us. The spirit of your amai will be able to find you."

Sam picked a blade of grass and stared down at it, at the tiny hairs running alongside the blade and the tiny teeth at its edge. In the dying light, the breeze stilled, and in that stillness the calls of children reached up to them. He remembered how when he called out "Amai!" in the secret place when he was frightened, he'd suddenly been able to find the way out.

"Your aunty is your amai's sister, isn't she?"

Sam nodded.

"So that means that there's some of your amai in her. And you are your amai's son, are you not?"

"Of course I am!"

"So she lives on in you, too. As does your atate. Your amai is with you always, Sam. She is in the secret place in your heart."

"Even though she's not buried here?"

"Even though she's not buried here. But she was here when she was a girl. And now you are here. You walk the tracks she walked, you see the things she saw, you smell the flowers and the earth that she smelled. She has left parts of herself here. Your mother was here, growing up with your aunt."

Suddenly, Sam had a sharp vision of his mother when she was his age. She looked a bit like Ezza and also a bit like him;

he imagined her and Aunty setting off down the track, going to fetch firewood as he had done.

"Your aunt is a good woman, you know. She loves you. And you have brothers and a sister now, too. You're not alone."

Sam nodded slowly into the gathering darkness. Around them crickets chirruped and sawed their song.

"Here." Allan passed him a bar of chocolate.

"For me?" It was the first time Sam had seen chocolate since at least a week before Amai died. He took off the wrapper, broke off a row of squares, and held it out.

Allan took a square. "Thank you. No more, though. The rest's yours."

Sam hesitated, then he wrapped the bar up again.

"Aren't you going to have any?"

Sam shook his head. "I'll save it to share with the others. . . . Aunty keeps calling me Sammy!" he said suddenly.

Allan laughed. "Does that matter?"

Sam found he was laughing then, too. "No. No, it doesn't."

They were silent again as dusk turned to dark.

"Amai!" Sam whispered into the air.

A wisp of warm breeze tickled his cheek in answer. He put his hand up to it and held it there.

"You can always come up here, you know," said Allan. "You don't need me to bring you. Your aunt will understand."

"Yes," said Sam.

Fires glowed like red pinpricks down on the plain, and the moon began to turn the land silver-gray.

"Come, Sam." Allan stood and put out a hand, and Sam took it.

25

"AS SOON AS I'VE TAKEN YOU HOME, I'LL RETURN THE laptop." They were back at the motorbike.

"No." Sam pulled away. "I want to walk there." To walk, not be taken. He'd left alone. He would return alone.

Allan gazed at him, then nodded slowly. "Very well. I'll bring your bundle when I've been at the hospital. Go now."

Outside every hut as Sam passed was the glow of a fire, and the air was full of the smells of food cooking. His tummy rumbled, he was so hungry. But as he turned the last corner to reach Aunty's, there was no fire; all he could see were shadowy figures. There were no sounds of supper; all he could hear were voices raised.

He took a deep breath, straightened his back, held his head high, flared his nostrils as Mansa Musa would have done, and walked on.

"Sam!" Two bodies hurled themselves at him, almost knocking the wind out of him. In the darkness he hadn't seen them coming. "Where were you? I wanted to ask if we could read your book together," said Enock.

"And then we saw it was gone!" cried Ezelina.

"And you didn't come when we called," said Enock, "and more of your things were gone, too."

Chikondi was toddling toward them. He grabbed Sam's leg. "Tham!" He toppled over.

Sam picked Chikondi up before the toddler's quivering lip gave way to a bawl of indignation. "Hello, there."

He got a toothy grin in response. "Tham."

Then Aunty was on them, too, but she wasn't smiling. She grabbed Sam by the arm. "Where have you been?" She shook him.

Ezelina quickly took Chikondi from Sam and set him down on the ground. The toddler stuck his thumb in his mouth and watched, eyes big and round.

"Where have you been? I come back from the doctors' and you are not here. I ask Ezelina if she knows where you are and she does not know. I ask Enock. He does not know. I ask Macdonald, I even ask Mavuto. Nobody knows. Where were you?" Her voice broke. "How could you go off like that without telling anyone? I've been out of my mind with worry!"

Sam looked nervously at her. There was a note in her voice that he hadn't heard before. She wasn't just cross; there was something else.

"And your books, your precious *Travels of Mansa Musa.* Where are they? What have you done with them?"

For a moment, Sam wasn't sure. Had he left them in the field? Then he remembered. "Allan's got them."

"Allan? Who is this Allan?"

"Allan Poot. The man with the motorbike, Amai," Ezelina explained.

"He's going to let us ride it," Enock said.

"He took Sam and me to the tea factory. We did tell you."

"So you did." She'd never stopped looking at Sam during the twins' interruption. "Did you give your books to this man?"

"They're in my bundle," he said, shaking his head.

"Your bundle!" She frowned. "And what has this Allan Poot to do with you and your bundle?"

"He found me and brought me back."

"Back from where exactly?"

"Oh!" But he couldn't say. He wouldn't. "I was on the track."

She gazed at him. "And where were you going?" Her voice was very low suddenly. "Where, Sammy? Answer me."

He gulped. "I was going away."

"Away? Oh, Sammy. But this is your home, here, with us."

A tear splashed out, and another. Sam lowered his head and howled.

In an instant strong arms were around him and holding him tight. She cradled him, rocked him against her, not speaking, not saying a word. That's how they stayed, as he cried and cried, a waterfall of tears. Against his head, he felt her chest vibrate as she began softly to croon a song, and she rocked him.

Slowly, his tears dried and his sobs turned to hiccupping. And then there was only the sound of her singing. Other hands touched him. "Tham?" he heard Chikondi again.

"Hush, Chik." Enock's voice.

He felt Aunt Mercy look up over his head, felt her shake her head. He stirred and turned round. There beside her stood Macdonald and Mavuto.

Sam stiffened.

"We have come to tell you something," said Macdonald.

Sam stared at them from the security of his aunt's arms. She relaxed her hold and pushed him very gently. He brushed his eyes with the back of his hand, sniffed hard, and faced them.

Macdonald, in turn, pushed Mavuto forward.

"I took your stupid shoes. It was me," Mavuto mumbled. He looked up. "Macdonald said you thought it was him. It wasn't. I did it. Macdonald got them off me. He said I shouldn't. And then you, you toe-rag, you never believed Macdonald."

Sam glanced at Macdonald, who nodded. "It's true."

"You never said."

"That's because he's my friend," Macdonald said simply.

"I'm sorry." Mavuto looked Sam right in the eye.

Aunt Mercy reached out and smoothed Sam's forehead. She hugged him, then let him go. "They are not bad boys," she said. Sam waited for her to say more, but she didn't.

Sam fumbled in his pocket. He took out the chocolate.

Six pairs of eyes watched his fingers as he broke it carefully into squares.

"Here." He handed the first square to Macdonald.

Macdonald nodded stiffly, put it in his mouth, and chewed. At first, his expression didn't change, then bit by bit the corners of his mouth began to lift.

"I'm sorry I called you a thief," Sam said.

"That's okay." The smile was slowly spreading to Macdonald's eyes.

Mavuto whooped for joy when he got his piece, the second.

"And me."

"And me."

Enock and Ezelina held out their hands.

"And the last one's for you." Sam popped it into Chikondi's mouth, which was already open and waiting like a young bird's.

"Come on, you lot!" Aunt Mercy clapped her hands together. "Macdonald! Lay the fire and light it. Here are some matches." She produced them from the pocket of her skirt. "I suppose you took the matches we had," she said to Sam.

He nodded. "I thought I might need them to light a fire."

Aunt Mercy turned away, but not before he'd seen the glimmer of a smile on her face. "Mavuto! You can help tonight. Enock—fetch the relish."

"Tell us where you went, we want to know," Enock demanded. "Did you have an adventure?"

"Enock, I'm not asking you twice."

"Come and fetch it with me, then, Sam."

"Oh, I just walked round a bit." Sam didn't want to tell them why he'd gone, or where. Then, boasting, as they entered the hut, "Actually, I got quite far."

"How far did you mean to go? Would you have got home again if the man hadn't brought you on his motorbike? We were really worried, weren't we, Ezza? Specially when it got dark. I mean, with you not knowing it so well around here as we do. And with the spirits walking at night."

"We were worried anyway," Ezelina said. "Why did you leave? Was it because of your amai? She's up there. We put her back on the shelf. Her photograph."

"She's beautiful, your amai," Enock said. "You know, your nose looks just like hers."

"And your eyes," Ezelina said. "Was it really just the two of you together after your atate died?"

Sam was surprised. She sounded interested and even, he thought, wistful.

They heard the rumble of a motorbike coming closer. Enock, about to rush out of the hut, bag of beans in his hand, stopped suddenly, so that Ezelina banged into him.

"Hey!" He pointed at Sam's feet. "Where are your shoes? Has someone stolen them again?"

Sam hesitated. He shook his head. "I lost them somewhere."

"Oh." Enock looked sad. Then his face lightened.

"Maybe a spirit saw them and took them," he suggested, following Sam and Ezelina out of the hut. "Maybe they'll turn up again like last time."

"Mmm." Sam smiled as he went toward the fire and supper. He didn't think they would.

Author's Note

If you would like to read about Mansa Musa, there is a book by Kephra Burns called *Mansa Musa: The Lion of Mali* (New York: Gulliver Books, 2001).

Sam's other favorite book, about an orphan, is *Oliver Twist* by Charles Dickens.

I should like to acknowledge *Land of Fire*, oral literature from Malawi, collected by J. M. Schoffeleers and A. A. Roscoe (Popular Publications, Limbe, Malawi). I took some extracts from their stories, and they are told here by the carpenter.

My thanks go to Henry and to Allan, and to my young readers, Adjoa, Alex, and Matt. Also to Jean-Christophe Boele van Hensbroek and Monique Postma for judicious and helpful advice.

Most of all, I am grateful to Bram and Sascha Sizoo, doctors a few years ago at the Mulanje Mission Hospital, without whom this book would not have been written.

In Malawi, as of this writing, about 14 percent of the population is infected with HIV, which leads to AIDS—"the Disease," as it is often called there—which attacks the patient's immune system. As patients weaken, they often succumb to tuberculosis and cough horribly, as Sam's mother and Brown do in this story. In some families, both parents die, leaving the oldest brother or sister to look after the younger children. If they are lucky, a relative or a neighbor will take them in and look after them.

Glossary

The italicized words are Chichewa, the language spoken in Sam's part of Malawi. The other words are commonly used in the countries of southern Africa or are simply English words used differently than in English.

amai	mom/mother
atate	dad/father
boma	local government center
calabash	the dried shell of a gourd, used as a bowl
the Disease	AIDS (Acquired Immune Deficiency Syndrome)
doekie	a scarf worn elaborately tied round a woman's head
kwacha	a Malawian coin
late	dead
mavuto	trouble
mealie meal	cornmeal
Muli bwanje	Hello, how are you?
nchimi	witch doctor
Ndili bwino	I'm well.
Ndili bwino, kaia inu	I'm well if you are well.

nsima	thick white corn "porridge," a Malawian dietary staple
sing'anga	someone expert in the use of herbs for many purposes, including medicine
tokolosh	a mischievous spirit, often scary
tumbu fly	a tropical fly that lays eggs in clothes. If you wear the clothes, the eggs may hatch under your skin (not pleasant). Ironing kills the eggs.
ululating	a high wailing sound made by women, usually in celebration or in mourning
zikomo	thank you